Sir Gawain
and the
Green Knight

Sir Gawain
and the
Green Knight

TRANSLATED AND
ILLUSTRATED
BY MICHAEL SMITH

Unbound

This edition first published in 2018

Unbound
6th Floor Mutual House, 70 Conduit Street, London W1S 2GF

www.unbound.com

Text design by PDQ Digital Media Solutions, Bungay, UK

A CIP record for this book is available from the British Library

ISBN 978-1-78352-560-7 (trade hbk)
ISBN 978-1-78352-561-4 (ebook)
ISBN 978-1-78352-562-1 (limited edition)

Printed in Great Britain by T J International

1 3 5 7 9 8 6 4 2

To my wife, Nicky
and our three children,
Monica, Beatrice and Hector

And for my mother, Margaret

Dear Reader,

The book you are holding came about in a rather different way to most others. It was funded directly by readers through a new website: Unbound. Unbound is the creation of three writers. We started the company because we believed there had to be a better deal for both writers and readers. On the Unbound website, authors share the ideas for the books they want to write directly with readers. If enough of you support the book by pledging for it in advance, we produce a beautifully bound special subscribers' edition and distribute a regular edition and ebook wherever books are sold, in shops and online.

This new way of publishing is actually a very old idea (Samuel Johnson funded his dictionary this way). We're just using the internet to build each writer a network of patrons. At the back of this book, you'll find the names of all the people who made it happen.

Publishing in this way means readers are no longer just passive consumers of the books they buy, and authors are free to write the books they really want. They get a much fairer return too – half the profits their books generate, rather than a tiny percentage of the cover price.

If you're not yet a subscriber, we hope that you'll want to join our publishing revolution and have your name listed in one of our books in the future. To get you started, here is a £5 discount on your first pledge. Just visit unbound.com, make your pledge and type **knight5** in the promo code box when you check out.

Thank you for your support,

Dan, Justin and John
Founders, Unbound

CONTENTS

In memory of Dr Marek Siemiradzki,
who so much supported this project:

And þus ȝirnez þe ȝere in ȝisterdayez mony,
And wynter wyndez aȝayn, as þe worlde askez,
no fage

INTRODUCTION

Sir Gawain and the Green Knight was written in the north-west of England in the late fourteenth century, during the reign of either Edward III (1327–77), Richard II (1377–99) or Henry IV (1399–1413), by an unknown hand. Whether the surviving manuscript was written by the poet himself or by a monastic scribe working on his behalf, it is nonetheless a masterpiece of beauty, mystery and suspense. Taking the form of an Arthurian romance, it employs alliteration to achieve its emphasis and poetic form, a technique whose origins stretch back to *Beowulf*, from the tenth century, and beyond. Alliteration experienced a revival in the fourteenth century, gaining particular favour in the west, Midlands and north of England in such works as *Piers Plowman*, *Wynnere and Wastoure* and other writing by the Gawain-poet himself. *Gawain* itself is a magical journey into a fabulous land, crafted with words as rich as any work written in the period and detailing the lives, rituals and natural environment of a world now lost to us. The vernacular dialect of the poet, his choice of story matter and the location in which the poem is set are all significant to an understanding of what the poem is about and its intended impact. Yet it also contains some fascinating secrets, which at first glance may not be evident; in particular, the way it seems to allude to the political landscape of the late fourteenth century.

Sir Gawain is a triumph of style, execution and plot and is divided into four distinct parts, or 'fitts'. The poem possesses a gripping dialogue, a wonderful sense of contemporary detail and excellent descriptive qualities, worthy indeed of a short story or novella. It tells the story of King Arthur's cousin who takes the place of the king in accepting the macabre challenge of a mysterious green horseman who comes to Camelot at Christmas. It is the Green Knight's survival, and Gawain's quest to find his nemesis at the Green Chapel, which forms the background to this astonishing tale. The challenges Gawain faces, and how he overcomes them, become the focus of the story, giving the reader a fascinating insight into mediaeval honour, morality and personal discipline. This study in the conflict between religious dedication, martial training and the duties of chivalric behaviour mean that *Sir Gawain* is more than just another story in the Arthurian canon; it is a manual on how a true knight should behave when faced with conflicting demands. It is for this reason that the Gawain-poet has come to be seen as a poet–mentor, perhaps to a king or powerful noble, compelling us to look at the poem's words and meaning in a whole new light.

Although it has been argued that many alliterative works of this period were written for private reflection, *Sir Gawain* was quite likely to have been produced with an audience in mind as well. For example, the poet moves us from the past tense to the present and back again to set the scene, draw us in and then lift us above the action. At times, he almost whispers to us, such as when he tells Gawain to think about the consequences of his actions at the end of Fitt 1. In Fitt 3 the poet throws us amongst the hunters when they dismember their catch by traditional rote – we can almost smell the bloody offal as it is cut, sliced and knotted. His playfulness when Lady Bertilak traps Gawain below the blankets in Fitt 3 is as funny as it is erotic. Throughout, the poet's exquisite grasp of the English language, most notably shown by his ability constantly to apply alliteration with new and varied words and techniques, reveals him to be a man of letters, form and purpose. He then embellishes this with his mesmerising use of the 'bob and wheel' technique at the end of each stanza to lift or lower the mood. Here, a line with an additional pair of syllables (the 'bob') introduces a pair of rhyming couplets (the 'wheel') to create a natural break in the narration. The use of this technique to carry the story, to remind us of a theme or to add suspense, reveals a storyteller immersed in art, technique and theatre. It also serves to give natural performance breaks in the work, supplemented of course by the division into four fitts, each with their own unique atmosphere to build suspense.

The Gawain-poet plays his own part too, acting as occasional narrator and revealing himself to his audience with phrases such as 'as I have heard tell' or 'as I've heard the book does say'. Yet we are none the wiser as to who he was in real life. Many theories have been advanced concerning the authorship of the poem, and the three other works bound together with it, *Pearl*, *Cleanness* and *Patience* (referred to collectively as Cotton Nero A.x, their classification number in the British Library). But despite much research, the poet still remains a mystery. However, we know from the dialect in which the poem was written that it was regional to the north-west Midlands. We also can surmise by the geographic references in the work that the poet was very familiar with the coast of North Wales, the Wirral and the hilly landscape of the Peak District and the Staffordshire Roaches, and the Green Chapel can be placed convincingly in this area.

The dialect and the geography assist in identifying the poet as a north-westerner. Although it is thought that many of the alliterative poets operated at a level below that of kings and dukes, the nature and quality of *Sir Gawain and the Green Knight* strongly suggest that he was well connected, probably serving either the Palatinate of Chester or the Duchy of Lancaster. There is also an indication that the poet placed the stories of King Arthur wilfully into this regional setting for local audiences. For example, in describing Camelot high on its hill, he might have been siting Arthur's court at the Cheshire castle of Beeston, situated on its lofty crag with views stretching many miles in all directions (see appendix 'In Search of Hautdesert'). The poet was writing for others who would have known the geographical basin of southern Lancashire, northern Cheshire and the flat expanse of the Cheshire Plain, surrounded by the Lancashire uplands, the Peaks and the Roaches. They most likely knew the coast of North Wales and, in travelling the coastal road with its famous Edwardian bastions from Flint to Caernarfon, would have known too the 'wilderness of Wirral' (line 701), which is visible as a great tongue of land from the old high road into North Wales. This was an area surrounded by hills, with its own distinct culture, legal system, family networks and dialect. *Sir Gawain and the Green Knight* would have resonated strongly with the landed and intellectual classes of a nationally powerful north-west.

But the poem is not an assertion of regional identity for its own sake. It follows very much the rules of many mediaeval stories by placing itself in an historical context to establish its authority. Hence, it begins by telling us that its story emerges from the Brut, the histories of Britain, which assert the land's origins stretching

4

right back to the siege of Troy and its subsequent establishment by Brutus. It reasserts this by reminding us at the end of the 'British books' (line 2523) and the literary tradition from which it has emerged. In common with other works, the poetic conceit was to ascribe to others the substantive 'idea' behind his work (in this case, the 'matter of Britain'), while it is the poet himself who then creates the 'sense' – the embellishment of the idea by means of true literary craft. The Gawain-poet tells us (lines 30–36) that he has heard the poem from others, as it's been so long in this land, and what he serves up is his personally crafted alliterative version of a well-established story.

The Gawain-poet was also a man of letters. In places, his style indicates he knew legal language and clearly that he was familiar not only with the broader trend of the alliterative revival but also with a broad corpus of works in the Arthurian tradition. He also understood military ritual, courtly behaviour, architecture and hunting. He borrows from other works in crafting his own poem (for example, his description of dismembering the deer in Fitt 3), yet he is no mere scrivener. He embellishes his writing with the flourishes of a master: pace, richness, suspense, poetry, credibility, and historic and contemporary substance.

If we view his work in the context of the other poems in the Cotton manuscript, we see that *Gawain* is unusual – although clearly part of the same corpus. *Pearl* is an exquisite and melancholy reflection on the loss of a daughter; *Patience* and *Cleanness* are more typical religious tracts. *Gawain*, on the other hand, appears more as a structured fiction and behavioural treatise, skilfully drawing together themes such as loyalty, kingship, discipline, vanity and selfishness. Yet it too has a religious bearing, with a strong focus on chastity. With this in mind, and reflecting on the poem's possible origins in one of the two great regional powerhouses of either Richard II or his uncle, John of Gaunt, we might then consider that the Gawain-poet was a poet–mentor for a senior lord, perhaps even the king. Hence, he would have been privy to great deeds and have operated at a level that was close to the political machinations at the very top of society. If we accept that the poem not only has geographical but also political links to Cheshire or Lancashire, an area with significant royal connections at the highest level, then we must also conclude that the poet believed in a powerful monarchy – one that could govern effectively.

Certainly, the stability of the realm was a key issue in England in the final quarter of the fourteenth century (and indeed in the Lancastrian years that followed the death of Richard II). Whether we reflect upon the decline of Edward III and the increasing power of his mistress Alice Perrers during his dotage, or upon the inexperience, or the later tyranny, of Richard II, his grandson and successor, we can see that the broader political scene was one of instability. Dealing with the importance of spiritual and moral discipline and highlighting its fragility when confronted with the dark power of temptation and deception (or when overlooked by unfettered pride and arrogance), the poem acts as a reflective commentary on effective leadership in troubled times. *Gawain* might be read as some form of instructional manual for effective kingship, acting as a guide to a monarch in how to confront and overcome multiple challenges. Hiding behind its glorious language and fabulous plot, the poem becomes a treatise on monarchical effectiveness. Depending on when it was written, it can be viewed as a contemporary reflection on the decline of Edward III; as a guide for young Richard II misled by powerful and detested friends; or possibly even as an allegory of, or apologia for, the deposition and death of Richard II at the hands of Henry Bolingbroke (Henry IV to be), who was recovering his lands following the death of his father, John of Gaunt. *Sir Gawain and the Green Knight* is not simply an Arthurian romance, but so much more.

Yet the Arthurian context is relevant, not least in enabling the poet to provide guidance without personal risk to himself. Certainly, these romances had blossomed in the fourteenth century, as shown most notably in the alliterative *Morte Arthure* of circa 1400 (contemporary with the rise of the house of Lancaster). The cult of Arthur, and that of chivalry itself, achieved its greatest expression during the period with Edward III's Order of the Garter, founded in 1348, and the Order of the Star, established shortly afterwards in France by Jean II. These fraternities were popular evocations of the Arthurian ethos by selected knights with a common aim. In 1399 Marshal Boucicaut established in France the Enterprise of the Green Shield with the White Lady, which was dedicated to the protection of women, while in 1430 Philip of Burgundy established the Order of the Golden Fleece, dedicated to the reverence of God and the maintenance of the Christian faith. The Arthurian, religious and allegorical language of the poem would have been well understood by its intended audience.

The context of England's north-west is also relevant in understanding why the poet might have written in this style. Lancaster was the seat of John of Gaunt; Cheshire the base of the Earl of Chester, heir apparent to the throne. Depending on the date of composition, we might read the poem in different political contexts. Professor F. Ingledew argued that it was written during the reign of Edward III and reflects in some degree the king's infidelities: Gawain represents the ideal of resisting temptation, which Edward apparently could not. Alternatively, the poem could be a metaphor for the decline of the chivalric ideal as Edward, the former great soldier, succumbed to the powers and flattery of Alice Perrers, thus dating the poem to later in his reign. Or the poet might have been writing from the court of John of Gaunt, Edward's second son and effectively guardian of England in the years between the death of the Black Prince (1376), and the ending of the minority of his son Richard II, in 1389. The parts played by Lady Bertilak and Morgan le Fay, combined with the misogynistic twist towards the end of the poem, may well be a reflection on events at the end of Edward's reign as seen from an uneasy Lancashire. *Gawain* becomes a warning to a future king about avoiding becoming ensnared by seduction – whether sexual or otherwise. In modern parlance, careless talk costs lives.

Yet we might choose to place the writing of the poem during the reigns of either Richard II or Henry IV. Then we could see *Sir Gawain and the Green Knight* as a political allegory directed at either leader. Here, the figure of the monarch – the king who can never die – is personified in the Green Knight himself, who cannot be killed; as the accession proclamation announces, 'The king is dead. Long live the king.' Could Gawain, in wielding the axe at Camelot but not being punished at the Green Chapel, be the person of Bolingbroke who has slain a king (Green Knight) but is absolved of his deeds? Is the poet's description of the 'surquedry' of the Round Table, its overweening pride, somehow a judgement on the court of Richard II and a statement that punishment (or death) can be the only reward for such arrogance and folly? Certainly, the poem's outcome is curious in the way that the Green Knight ultimately forgives Gawain – suggesting in this scenario that we should forgive Bolingbroke. Indeed, we are almost sorry for the Green Knight as a lost soul at the end, returning to who knows where. Is it possible that a rueful Green

Knight is himself an apologist for grim deeds and stands as a dutiful ally of a necessary act by Bolingbroke to preserve the institution of monarchy lest it collapse?

The ghostly aspect and colour of the Green Knight – the colour of a devilish underworld – is also instructive. Are we being asked instead to consider him as some form of ghoulish reincarnation of Edward III's greatest years or maybe even that of the Black Prince, himself denied the crown by an early demise and perhaps seen here as the true martial king that England should have had instead of Richard? Or is the Green Knight instead the ghost of Richard himself? We know that Richard, like Bertilak, had a deep love of hunting and a profound and respectful love for his wife, Anne of Bohemia. Is the Green Knight, Bertilak's shape-shifting alter ego, the ghost of Richard who is shown to forgive the deeds of Bolingbroke in order to legitimise him in the eyes of the great courts of the English north?

Yet Gawain's journey through North Wales appears to argue the contrary. Just as Richard landed in South Wales in 1399 and then travelled by an obscure route (until chroniclers flesh out the detail of his journey later), so too does Gawain follow a route from Camelot, which begins to be described only when he reaches North Wales. In mirroring the travels of Richard II, Gawain becomes instead the young king, journeying to face down his challenger Bolingbroke, in the form of the Green Knight. The Green Chapel itself is curious, having as it does multiple entrances; not unlike the central hall in the donjon, or keep, of Flint, where the king met Bolingbroke at the end of his own Welsh journey.

Gawain, in surviving his meeting with the Green Knight, returns to Camelot at least as moral victor while rueing his sins. Yes, he has failed, he is ashamed of his failings, he wonders if he can change, yet he is reassured by the court that he is welcome back home. He has somehow been cleansed and has also, perhaps, purified his arrogant court by his deeds. If the poet's Camelot is Beeston, then Gawain's cleansing return is celebrated in its rightful place: a seat of the Earls of Chester, first sons of the reigning monarch. The poem then appears as a contemplative guide addressed to a youthful, misguided monarch who needs to change. If the poem is a reflection on these acts, it may have been compiled in that short time between Richard II's return from Ireland in July 1399 and his untimely demise at Pontefract in February 1400. The poet may well have hoped that the true king would not be deposed.

Of course, this can only be speculation as we cannot establish an accurate date for the poem. History, and the Gawain-poet himself, has chosen to hide from us any details for the identification of date or author, and we have no documentary evidence either. However, we do know that alliterative poetry flourished in a revival in the fourteenth century and was practised largely by poets in the west, north-west and north of England, and also in Scotland. Chaucer's Parson dismisses the alliterative style when he says,

> But trusteth wel, I am a Southren man,
> A kan nat geeste 'rum, ram, ruf', by lettre.

Written between 1387 and 1400, *The Canterbury Tales* reveals in this small detail that in the north, a form of poetry was practised that was anathema to the 'Southren man', or rather to the upper echelons of southern society, be they officials, knights or other senior figures. Professor T. Turville-Petre, in *The Alliterative Revival*, argues that the relatively poor quality of surviving manuscripts of alliterative poetry (in terms of the way they were bound and illustrated) implies that they were enjoyed at a rank below the nobility and were, in a way, aspirational. While the Cotton manuscript, with its attempts at illumination, appears sophisticated alongside its contemporaries in the alliterative revival, it is less so when compared to the spectacular Ellesmere *Canterbury Tales*, and similar major survivors. Yet for alliterative poems to be so well known – and referred to by Chaucer himself – implies that they were enjoyed in the late fourteenth century; some, such as *Piers Plowman*, had a very broad readership at this time. Indeed, it is the fact that *Gawain* appears to be aimed at an audience which understood military matters, courtly behaviour and hunting rituals that enables us to be able to arrive at a date almost contemporary with Chaucer.

While some of the poems in the revival, for example, *Wynnere and Wastoure*, make direct references to Edward III and the Order of the Garter, *Sir Gawain and the Green Knight* is less forthcoming, although it does conclude with the motto of the Order (albeit written in a different hand). However, the poem's attention to detail furnishes us with more subtle – yet no less relevant – clues. Perhaps the most direct is the description of Gawain's armour in Fitt 2, which can be dated to between 1360 and 1410, between the English victories at Crécy (1346) and Poitiers (1356) and that of Agincourt (1415). The description matches almost perfectly the armour of knightly effigies and brasses, such as those of late-fourteenth-century figures, such as John de la Pole, Thomas de Audley and Reginald de Cobham, and by 1410 the style was dying out. (See 'Glossary of Armour'.)

We are also given fascinating clues for the date when the Gawain-poet describes the mysterious castle of Hautdesert, not so much a military stronghold but a homestead within a landscaped setting. The castle appears within its park, palisaded all around, presumably in the manner of a deer park so typical of lordly households even up until the eighteenth century, when such places were still identified by their parks on the earliest county maps. The poet describes features that are not military but ornate, and the castle emerges from water, which appears to double the height of the building. Hautdesert is part of a new, more subtle form of castle being built across the land in the latter part of the fourteenth century by lords returning wealthy from campaigns in France. Instead of Dover, Harlech or Windsor, we imagine more magical aesthetic homestead castles such as Nunney, Bodiam or Caister in Norfolk. The inspiration for Hautdesert – and some of the extra clues revealed by an examination of it – is provided in the appendix 'In Search of Hautdesert'.

The Cotton manuscript also acts as a dating guide because it contains a number of illuminations which are either contemporary with it or were added only a few years after the poem was written and help to establish an overall date for the poem of the second half of the fourteenth century. Turville-Petre is rightly dismissive of their quality when he says they are 'dreadful, and they have been described – with pardonable exaggeration – as "infantile daubs"'. While this is true, they are nonetheless informative on a general dating. Men wear the distinctive twin-forked beard of the later fourteenth century; their hair is brushed to sweep outwards; the Green Knight wears the tightly fitting outfit so typical of the period; even the illuminated letters are reminiscent of those accompanying the Agincourt Carol of 1415. We must view these illustrations as we might look upon ancient laws – seeing not the law itself but what it legislates *against*.

Sir Gawain and the Green Knight stands out as a masterpiece not only of Middle English but also of English literature. It embraces a host of different themes, many of which are graphically descriptive, and others mythical, religious, supernatural, metaphorical and even existential. The mastery of technique is such that the Gawain-poet blends the intensity of religious fervour, the humour of chivalric politesse, the melancholy of the passing year and the brutality of the hunt with equal measure. Just as he can give Lady Bertilak huge erotic power, he can also humiliate the chivalric ideal. While he crafts Gawain's sophisticated 'love-talking', he can cast the hero into dark, cold places of fear and loneliness. As he can cypher the sweet nothings of the batted eye, so he can brutally sever the head or slice the flesh of man and beast. He is a master storyteller and poet in one.

Whoever the author was, whatever his motivations, the quality of his writing, his flexibility of metaphor and his acute powers of description show that he was a man of culture. Although techniques employed in the poem were used in other works in the alliterative canon, there can be no doubt that the poet not only possessed great technical mastery but also understood the craft of literature itself, drawing from a wide range of sources and poetic influences. His gifted legacy tells us that English, far from being a backward language used only by the masses, was flowering at this time. Compared to earlier literature, the English language of the late fourteenth century was blossoming, cultured and – in the days before a common national language – regional in its practice, and honed as such for local unity and enjoyment.

Whether we see the poem as a reflection on a land in decay, as advice for a monarch or as political allegory, above all *Sir Gawain and the Green Knight* is a literary and poetic masterpiece, and one in which the poet conveyed just how good he was. His work remains one of the finest, arguably *the* finest, of the alliterative works to survive from the period and is indeed more than 'just' an alliterative poem. Yet tantalisingly, the poet is stubborn in his modesty: he neglects to tell us to whom it was that such genius should truly be ascribed. Perhaps, as a senior official in a land where monarchy was at that time unstable and alliances uncertain, he wished no one to know his name. But anonymity is not at all unusual in writings of this time. Possibly, like many other alliterative poets, the conceit was always to remain nameless for reasons unknown (save on rare occasions such as in the case of *Piers Plowman* by William Langland). The Gawain-poet's caution served to promote the works of others, like Chaucer, over a man who could almost be described not only as a great poet but also, like Chrétien de Troyes, as one of the first real novelists. But anonymity does not diminish greatness, his genius shines still and we honour him just the same. Like some ghostly wraith blowing coolly past us in a darkened corridor, he touches our shoulder and kisses our ear, but when we turn he is gone.

THE SURVIVAL OF THE POEM

The survival of *Sir Gawain and the Green Knight* and the other poems of the Cotton manuscript is remarkable. We do not know who commissioned it, who wrote the manuscript, whether it had more than one owner or whether it was mentioned in a will as an important asset. For more than 200 years, it survived in complete obscurity, only acquiring its current name after Sir Frederick Madden and Richard Morris brought their editions into print in the nineteenth century. All that we can be sure of is that the almost pocket-sized Cotton Nero A.x manuscript was once part of the library of Sir Henry Savile (1568–1617) of Banke, near Halifax in the West Riding of Yorkshire, and it was acquired by the collector Sir Robert Cotton (1571–1631), whose library of manuscripts outshone even those of England's monarchs. Britain owes a huge debt of gratitude to such collectors, who possessed both the personal interest and the foresight to find, purchase and preserve such works for posterity. For both *Beowulf* and *Sir Gawain and the Green Knight*, there is only a single surviving copy.

Such private libraries were significant. Following the dissolution of the monasteries under Henry VIII, great collections of works simply disappeared. John Aubrey, the antiquarian, speaks of his school books in the 1630s being bound with the pages of old volumes from local monasteries that had been dissolved by the king. For those unable to afford the services of a bookbinder, old parchment would have been a cheap source of binding materials. We can only guess at the scale of the loss wrought to Britain's literary heritage. Alongside complete surviving masterpieces in Middle English, scholars have come across many fragments of larger works, the remainder of which have long since disappeared.

On Robert Cotton's death, the library passed down to his son and then to John, his grandson, who, via acts of Parliament, was able to secure the collection for the nation so that, upon his death in 1702, it was to become the basis of today's British Library. Yet even at this point, disaster nearly struck. In 1731 Ashburnham House, where the new library held its collections, caught fire and many manuscripts were lost for ever. (*Beowulf* was badly damaged in the flames and came close to being destroyed.) The role of the Cotton family in the creation of this collection is still reflected in the use of his own archiving system based on the names of different Roman emperors.

A NOTE ON THIS TRANSLATION

My interest in *Sir Gawain and the Green Knight* stems from my own origins in the north-west of England and my particular interest in mediaeval history, stemming from my undergraduate days at the University of York. In undertaking this translation, I wanted to retain the rich, courtly language of the original, in addition to its evident regional bias. Occasionally, where words still exist in the local dialect (such as *threap* and *gry*), or where words work better without translation (such as *guisarme* or *blauner*), these have been retained. In all such cases, the reader is referred to the glossaries. I have also provided notes to enable the reader to decipher some of the contemporary meanings behind the poem (for example, references to the legends of King Arthur's court or descriptions of saints or of armour). A dagger at the end of the line alerts the reader to these notes. For ease of reference, the poem also retains the line numbering of the Early English Text Society edition of 1940, which will help the reader to locate the lines in the original Middle English.

In terms of my approach, I have not sought to assert an aggressive regionalism in the translation nor have I tried to be clever in the use of poetic language itself. Rather, I have tried to follow the language and rhythm of the original, and write as I hear it being spoken if the poet were to come back today. This is not as easy as it sounds. The original manuscript is not blessed with intelligible punctuation and nor is the use of verbs necessarily appropriate to how we would write today. Equally, pronunciation of the vowels was different (both within and at the end of some words) which would have created a distinct sense of rhythm and leads to significant problems for the translator in attempting to replicate both the rhyme and the flow while retaining the poet's own voice.

Wherever possible, I have also tried to follow the original alliteration in order to retain some of the aural elements of the poem. The alliteration may follow the conventional form (words beginning with the same letter or sound), or it may use the techniques of the Gawain-poet himself, where some of the alliteration comes in the form of sounds or letters within another word (for example, some words in a line may begin with 'w' while others might sound like a 'w', such as the 'o' in 'only'). I have also employed the variation between past and present tense which gives the original poem both its charm and its wonderful capability for suspense and action.

Throughout, I have also attempted to recreate the poet's method of incorporating a caesura, or pause, in each line, a technique stretching back to *Beowulf* and beyond. For example,

This king lay at Camelot [caesura] upon Christmas time

18

Depending on the line structure and number of syllables, the caesura occurs in different places, as it does in the original. Occasionally, this may require an emphasis on an unexpected syllable in order to retain the metre. In essence, my work is a modernised version of the poem, designed – I believe like the original – to be read aloud in a large hall for the enjoyment of others. Consequently, it often reads with some pace.

Finally, the poem also includes a selection of my own linocut prints which draw on the themes of the poem and attempt to be true to the descriptions given in the text. In producing these images, I have paid careful attention to mediaeval manuscripts and, in particular, those which were produced in the late fourteenth century – including, of course, the rather naïve illustrations which accompany the original poem in the Cotton manuscript. The illuminated letters that feature in this book are based on those in that manuscript and are also produced and printed using the same linocut process. They appear as they do throughout that wonderful document – at the beginning of each fitt and at key places throughout the text.

Sir Gawain
and the
Green Knight

FITT 1

So, when the siege and the assault was ceased at Troy,
And that burgh broken and burned to brands and ashes,
The traitor who wrought there every trace of treason
Was tried for his treachery, the truest on earth.
Thus it was Aeneas, the lord, and his high kind,   5
Who then oppressed provinces with power to become
The wealthiest of the wealthy in the western isles.
Romulus the rich raises Rome swiftly,
And quickly begets that borough with brilliance,
And with his name he names it, which it still has;   10
Ticius in Tuscany begins to build towers,
Langobard in Lombardy lifts up homesteads,
And there over the French flood, Felix Brutus
On many banks full broad, Britain he sets†

    within,   15
   Where war and wrack and wonder
   Have since occurred therein,
   And oft both bliss and blunder
   Full swift have shifted since.

And when that rich noble begat this place Britain,   20
Bold-bred they were there and lovers of battle
Who many times that came to pass brought trouble.
Famed feats have fallen in its lands more often
Than in any other that I know, ever since that very time.
But of all the kings that built here in Britain   25
The highest was Arthur, as I have heard tell.
So an adventure from here I aim to disclose,
That astounds some men still and grips them fast,
A stunning adventure from the legends of Arthur.
If you will listen to this tale but one little while   30
I shall tell it as tightly as I in turn heard it,
      by tongue;
  As it's been set and cast
  Into a story stout and strong;
  With linked letters thus held fast,   35
  In this land it's been so long.

This king lay at Camelot upon Christmas time,
With many of his lovely lords, lads of the best,
A right royal brethren of the Round Table,
With rich revel all right and reckless mirth.   40
These top men did tourney a good many times
And jousted with jollity, these most gentle knights,
Then clip-clopped to court, carolling to make.
For there the feast was like full fifteen days,
With all the meat and mirth that men could muster.   45
Such glamour and glee, glorious to hear,
A din upon day and dancing by night,
All was happy to the highest in hall and chamber
With lords and ladies a-lifting their thoughts!
With all the wealth of the world, they wined together,   50
The best-known knights in all Christendom
And the loveliest ladies that ever have lived,
And he, the comeliest king that court had beheld.
For all this fair folk were in their first prime and
        more still,   55
    Were the happiest under heaven,
    Their king the highest man of will;
    It is hard now to imagine
    More so hale as on this hill.

And then the realm ran forth, reaching for presents,
Seized their gifts on high and held them by hand;

While New Year was yet that it was just new born,   60
The doughty that day were doubly served on the dais.
For the king was coming with his knights to the hall,
And the chanting in the chapel had chuckled to an end;
Loud cries were cast there from clerics and others,
'Noel' announced anew, named full often.   65
And then the realm ran forth, reaching for presents,
Seized their gifts on high and held them by hand;
And about those gifts, the debate was busy!
Ladies laughed full loud – even those that lost –[†]
And he that won, he was not woeful; that you can believe!   70
All this mirth they made till mealtime;
When they had washed as due, they went to sit,
The best nobles high above, as so best it seemed.
Then Guinevere, full gay, graced their midst,
Dressed on the dais, adorned all about   75
With small silks besides, below a bright canopy
Of tried Toulouse and choice Tharsian tapestry,
Embroidered and bejewelled with the very best of gems –
No mere pennies were spent on those precious jewels
     that day!   80
  But the best ones on that queen?
  The glint of her eyes grey.
  Such similar can rare be seen
  So many men do say.

Then Guinevere, full gay, graced their midst,
Dressed on the dais, adorned all about
With small silks besides, below a bright canopy
Of tried Toulouse and choice Tharsian tapestry

But Arthur would not eat till all were served,   85
He was jolly in his joyfulness and somewhat childlike,
He liked active living, and loved it much less
When lying at length or sitting for longer,
So busied was he by young blood and wild brain.
And another manner also moved him thus,   90
Though noble by nurture he would never eat
Upon such a dear day, lest he were advised
Of some adventurous thing or an untold tale,
Of some mighty marvel that he might think true,
Of ancestors, arms and other adventures,   95
Or one of his men sought another strong knight
To join him in jousting, in jeopardy to lay
His own life for a life, living one or the other
As fortune would favour the fairer to have.
This was the king's custom when sat with his court,   100
At each flowing feast with his fellows in
        that hall;
    He was of face so fair,
    Most nobly standing tall,
    And so youthful in New Year   105
    Making mirth with one and all.

Thus there in his stall stands that stout king himself,
Talking of trifles before the high table;
There, good Gawain graced Guinevere's side,
And Agravain of the Hard Hand on the other side sits,   110
Both the king's nephews and full sturdy knights;
Bishop Baldwin begins as head of the table,
Then Yvain, son of Urien, eats sat beside him;
They were decked on that dais and most dutifully served,
And then many stout souls along the sidetables.   115
Then comes the first course with the cracking of trumpets,
With banners full bright which also behung them,
Now noisy nakers with those noble pipes,
Making such wild warbles and wakening loudness,
That many hearts heaved full high at their touch.   120
Delicate meat to delight is delivered,
A field of freshness, fashioned on dishes
That pine for a place before all the people,
Where silver bowls of hot stew may be severally set on
      the cloth;   125
   Each lord, he served himself
   And selected without sloth,
   Each two had dishes twelve –
   Good beer and bright wine both!

Now concerning that supper will I say no more,   130
For either way you will know that they wanted for nothing.
For another noise now, unknown, neared betimes,
That the king might be lucky to collect all his food;
For the moment the music was not much while ceased,
And the first course in that court so kindly served,   135
That there hails at the hall door a most awful man,
The highest beyond measure of the men at that meal;
From his stare to his shanks so stout and so thick,
And his legs and his limbs so long and so great,
Half-giant in that land I'd happen he were;   140
But a man I'm most minded still yet to be,
Though massive, the merriest that we might see ride;
For of back and of breast all, his body was strong,
Both his womb and his waist were worthily small,
And all his features corresponding to his form,   145
     full clean.
  Yet wonder at his hue men had,
  What did his semblance mean?
  He was a man like faerie clad:
  Entirely forest green!   150

And all geared in green was this giant and his wear,
A straight coat, full-stretched, that stuck to his sides,
A muffled mantle above, matched within too
With pure pelts apparent, picked out full clean,
With blithe, brushed blauner on both body and hood,   155
That was lying from his locks and was laid on his shoulders;
Well-hugging hose he wore of that same green,
That clasped both on his calves and under clean spurs,
Of bright gold on silk borders so richly banded,
And shoeless under shanks were his soles in the stirrups;   160
And verily verdant were the rest of his vestments,
Both the bars of his belt and the blithe stones,
That were richly arranged on his clothes and arrayed
About himself and his saddle; of its silken work
It would task me to tell of just half of those trifles   165
Embroidered about it with butterflies and birds,
And gay gaudy of green picked out in gold;
The pendants of his peytral and the proud crupper,
His mullets and the metal were all thus enamelled,
The stirrups that he stood on were stained of the same,   170
And his saddle bows all after, and his lordly skirts,
Ever glimmered and glinted all of green stones!
That fair mount that he fares on was fine-finished likewise for
    certain:
  A green horse great and thick,   175
  A steed full stiff to train;
  In embroidered bridle, quick –
  But to his master, easy game!

Well gay was this gentleman got up in green,
With the hair of his head matching that of his horse   180
Like fair fanning flax flowing over his shoulders;
A mighty beard like a bush hangs over his breast,
That with his long hair reaches down from his head,
And was clipped right all round just above his elbows,
So that half his arms under it were harnessed just like   185
That of a king's cape circling close round his neck.
The mane of that mighty horse was much like that too –
Well curled and combed with knots full many,
Folded with filidore about the fair green,
At once hitched with hair, yet again hitched with gold;   190
The tail and his top knot twin-trimmed to match,
And both of them bound with a band of bright green,
Daubed with dear stones where they docked the hair;
And then twisted by thong in a tight knot aloft,
Where many bright bells of burnished gold rang.   195
Such a fine-furnished horse no fellow has ridden,
Nor ever seen in this setting such a sight before then
      by eyes;
   He stared as fire burns bright,
   So said all who did him size;   200
   It seemed as no man might
   From his blows come through and rise.

Yet he had no helm nor no hauberk neither,
Nor no pysan nor no plate, appertaining to armour,
Nor no shaft, nor no shield to shove or to smite.   205
But in his hand he held a holly bough,
That is greatest in green when the greenwood is bare,
And an axe in his other hand, huge and immense,
A sure spiteful slicer if it could be so called;
The length of an ell-rod was that large head,   210
The groin of green steel and of golden hew,
The blade burnished brightly, with a broad edge
As well shaped to sheer as the sharpest of razors;
The stock of that stiff shaft which that strong man gripped
Was wound round with iron to the wand's end,   215
And with gracious workmanship engraved all in green;
A lace lapped about it that looped at the head,
And then down the handle, hitched full often
With well-tested tassels thereto tightly attached
With buttons of braid, bright green and full rich.   220
That horseman, he proceeds and enters the hall,
Drives to the high dais with no doubt nor no fear,
And he hails no one, looking high over heads.
His first words that awoke: 'Where is,' he said
'The governor of this gang? Gladly I would   225
See that soul myself, and with him reason
        alone!'
    And on those knights he cast his eye,
    And ruled them up and down;
    He stopped to study and to spy   230
    Which one there held most renown.

There was much lengthy looking to behold that lord,
For each man he marvelled at what it might mean
That a man and his horse might have such a hue
And grow green as the grass, and greener it seemed, 235
Than green enamel on gold – and glowing brighter.
Standing, they studied him, then slowly drew nearer,
With all the wonder of the world at what he would do.
For many marvels had they seen, but never such as this,
For he was some phantom or faerie or so those folk deemed; 240
Therefore those stout fellows did fear to answer,
And stone-still they sat, all stunned at his statement
In shushed silence throughout that whole knightly sitting;
Like all had slipped into sleep so slaked was their noise
      on high; 245
  Though I deem it not for fear
  Nor for manners gone awry;
  For the king, their overseer,
  Was the man who should reply.

Then Arthur beholds him before the high dais,   250
And reverenced him royally, for he was not afraid,
And said, 'We wish warm welcome to you in our place,
The head of this hostelry, Arthur I am;
So please, alight lovingly and linger a while,
And what so is your will, we shall grant it after.'   255
'No, so help me,' said the man, 'by He upon high,
To dwell a while in this way was not my errand;
But the light of you, lord, which renown lifts so high,
And whose borough and noblemen are best beheld,
The sturdiest in steel who do ride on their steeds,   260
The wisest and worthiest of the world's kind,
Yet valiant at play and other pure sports,
And where found is kind courtesy as I have heard spoken,
All this wends me here, right now at this time.
You may be sure by this branch which I bear here   265
That I pass in peace and no peril seek;
For had I journeyed here in fighting form,
I have a hauberk at home and a helmet both,
A shield and a sharp spear shining bright,
And other weapons to wield, I might also wonder;   270
But these I don't want, for what I wear is softer.
But if you be so bold as most nobles do tell,
You will graciously grant me the game that I ask
        by right.'
    And Arthur, he did swear,   275
    And said, 'Sir courteous knight,
    If you crave "battle bare"
    You'll not fail to get a fight.'

38

'No, I favour no fight, in faith I tell you,
For there's naught on this bench but beardless children!   280
If I were hasped all in armour and on my high horse,
There'd be no man to match me, their might is so weak!
Thus I crave of this court a Christmas game,
For it is Noel and New Year and here are young bucks;
And if any in this hall holds himself to be hardy,   285
Be he bold in his blood or may be bull-headed,
That would stiffly swap one stroke for another,
I shall grant him this guisarme as a great gift,
This axe, whole and heavy, to wield as he likes,
And I shall bide the first blow as bare as I sit.   290
If any fellow be so fierce to fare as I ask,
Let him leap light to me and latch onto this weapon –
I quit-claim it forever, he can keep it as his –
And I shall stand him one stroke, stiff on this floor,
Provided you deign me to deal his doom the   295
    same way;
  Yet I'll give him some respite
  Of twelve months and a day;
  So, lords, please don't sit tight,
  Who here has aught to say?'   300

If he astounded them first, all stunned were they now
All that hall's household, the high and the low;
The rider on his rouncey rose in his saddle,
And enraged he rolled his red eyes all about,
Bent his bristled brows, blinking all green,   305
And waved his beard to wait for whoso would arise.
When none would come to carp, he coughed with contempt,
Barking rime richly and rises to speak:
'What! Is this Arthur's house,' then said that horseman,
'That whose renown runs through so many realms?   310
Where now is your surquedry and conquering power,†
Your Grendel-wind, growling and all your great words?†
Now is the Round Table, its renown and its revelling,
Overturned with a word of one man's speech;
For all shrink with shaking without a blow shown!'   315
With this he laughs so loud that the lord was aggrieved;
The blood shot for shame to his face, cheeks
          and ears;
     He waxed with wrath in mind,
     As did all those that were here,   320
     The king, so keen by kind
     Then by that man stood near.

And said, 'Horseman, by heaven, your asking is nice,
And as folly you seek, so fate you shall find;
I know no good knight aghast at your great words.   325
Give me your guisarme, upon God's will,
And I shall beget that boon which you bid me do!'
He leaps up politely and lays out his hand;
Then fiercely on foot alights that green fellow.
Now Arthur has the axe and thus grips the handle,   330
And stirs it sternly about, as if thinking to strike.
But that stiff man before him just stood straight and tall,
The highest in that house by a head or more;
With a stern stare he stood, stroking his beard,
And unmoved in his countenance he draws down his coat,   335
No more mithered nor dismayed by almighty blows
Than if any noble on that bench had becalmed him
     with wine.
  Gawain sat by the queen,
  To the king he did incline,   340
  'I beseech, avoid a scene;
  Let this melée please be mine.'

'Would you, worthy lord,' said Gawain to the king,
'Bid me budge from my bench and stand by you there,
So that I without villainy might void this table,   345
And that if my liege lady did not dislike it,
I would come to consult you, before your rich court.
For I think it unseemly, if the truth be known,
That such royal requests be addressed in this room,
And that you should be tempted to take up this task,   350
When there are those bold about you that sit on their benches,
That under heaven, I hope, are none higher of will,
Nor better at battling when bloodshed abounds;
I am the weakest, I know, and also the feeblest,
And less loving of my life if truth be told,   355
And am only praiseworthy since you are my uncle,
Your blood in my body being my only bounty;
And since this business is base and does not become you,
And as I asked you first, it should fall to me fairly;
And if my claim is not comely, then let this court choose, with 360
    no blame.'
  Then that realm it gathered round,
  And they all agreed the same,
  To relieve that king with crown,
  And give Gawain the game.   365

Then commanded the king for that knight to rise;
And he readily arose and made himself ready,
Knelt down by the king who conveys him that weapon;
Relinquished to him with love as he lifted his hand,
And gives him God's blessing and gladly bids him   370
That his heart and his hand should both be hardy.
'Take care, cousin,' said the king. 'that you make just one chop,
And if you read it right, readily I trust
That you shall bide any blow which he shall bring after.'
Gawain gets to the game, guisarme in hand,   375
And boldly abides, abashed not at all.
Then that knight in the green, he calls to Gawain,
'Let's repeat all our rules before we go further,
And first tell me, high sir, how it is that you hail,
You must tell me truly, so I may trust you.'   380
'In good faith,' shouts that good knight, 'Gawain I am called,
That brings you this blow, whatever befalls me
This time twelve months hence when another I take,
With what weapon you will, and from no one else
    alive.   385
  That other one swears again,
  'Sir Gawain, as I do thrive,
  So I am fairly fain
  To take the blow that you shall drive.'

'Take now that grim blade to you
And let's see how you knock.'
'Gladly, sir, I do,'
Said Gawain, stroking its stock.

'By God,' said the Green Knight, 'Gawain, you please me   390
That I shall feel from your fist what I have asked for;
And you have readily repeated by reason full true,
And cleanly, the covenant I asked of your king,
Save that, please assure me truthfully, sir,
You shall seek me by yourself, where so you hope   395
I may be found on firm earth, and fetch you such wages
As you deal me this day before this doughty realm.'
'Where should your walls be?' said Gawain. 'Where is your place?
By Him that wrought me, I know not where you dwell,
Nor do I know you, knight, your court nor your name.   400
But teach me truly those things, and tell me how you hail,
And I shall wear out my wits to win me straight there,
And that I swear to you truthfully, and by my assured troth.'
'That is for New Year, it needs no more for now,'
Said that giant in green to Gawain the noble,   405
'For I'll tell you truly when your tap I do take,
And you have smitten me smoothly, smartly I'll teach you
Of my house, my home and my own name,
Then you may ask of my welfare and keep our covenant,
And if I spend no speech now, then speeds you the better,   410
Or you could lounge in your land and look no further, but
        I mock!
    Take now that grim blade to you
    And let's see how you knock.'
    'Gladly, sir, I do,'   415
    Said Gawain, stroking its stock.

The Green Knight prepares, gravely on the ground;
With a little lowering of the head he lets all see the flesh.
His long, lovely locks he laid over his crown
So the naked neck to the nape showed.   420
Gawain gripped his axe and gathers it on high,
With his left foot on the floor, which he set before him,
Then let it down deftly to alight on that neck
So the sharp of that slicer splintered the bones,
And sank through the shining flesh, and so split it in two   425
That the bite of that bright steel bit on the ground.
The fair head from his shoulders hit to the earth
So that folk with their feet footed it around;
The blood brayed from the body and blotted the green
But neither faltered nor fell did that fellow, nor sink down,   430
But stoutly he starts forth upon his stiff shanks,
And, roaring, reached out there as all the ranks stood,
Laid hands on his lovely head and lifts it up sharply,
Then, huffing to his horse, the bridle he catches,
Steps into the stirrup and swings aloft,   435
And his head in his hand he holds by the hair;
And serenely that soul in his saddle sat
As if no mishap had ailed him, though headless he were
     instead!
  He bustled his bulk about,   440
  That ugly body that bled;
  Many, of him, had doubts
  When they thought of what he'd said.

For the head in his hand, he then holds up,
Addressing his face to those dear on the dais,   445
And he lifts up his eyelids and looked full abroad,
And didn't mince much with his mouth, as you'll hear.
'Look, Gawain, now get ready to do as you pledged,
And, lord, look for me loyally until you shall find me,
As you have promised in this hall and hereunto these knights.   450
So I charge you to choose the road to the Green Chapel, to fetch
Such a dent as you dealt and deserve,
To be yielded by contract on New Year's morn;
The Knight of the Green Chapel is how many know me;
And you'll not fail to find me if you ask of my name,   455
Therefore do come, or a coward be called, as you wish.'
With a raging rush of the reins, he turns,
And hailed out of the hall door, his head in his hand,
So that fire as from flint flew from all those fast hooves.
From what kith he came, no one there knew,   460
No more than they knew to where he was wending.
        What then?
    The king and Gawain there
    At the Green Knight laughed again;
    He was spoken of full bare   465
    As a marvel by those men.

For the head in his hand, he then holds up,
Addressing his face to those dear on the dais,
And he lifts up his eyelids and looked full abroad,
And didn't mince much with his mouth, as you'll hear.

Though Arthur that high king held awe in his heart,
He kept his thoughts secret, but he said full high
To his comely queen, with most courteous speech,
'Dear Dame, this day must never dismay you;   470
For it well becomes such craft upon Christmas,
As like a lull in the laughter and singing
And most kindly carolling of our knights and ladies;
Nonetheless, to my meal must I now attend,
Now I have seen my wonder, I dare not deny it.'   475
Then he glanced at Sir Gawain and gamely he said,
'Now, sir, hang up your axe, it's had enough hewing.'
And it was put to dangle above the dais on the doser to hang,
For all men to marvel at, who might care so to look,
And by true title thereof to tell of that wonder.   480
Then they busied to the tables, those nobles together,
The king and the good knight were both keenly served
Of all dainties double as befalls such dear men,
With all manner of meat and minstrelsy both;
With warm wealth they passed that day, till it wound to an end   485
    on land.
  Now think well, Sir Gawain,
  Of the danger you can't command
  From this adventure so obtained
  That you have taken in hand.   490

FITT 2

This gift grants Arthur the best of adventures,
To bless the New Year as he'd long yearned to hear;
Though words were wanting when they first went to sit,
Being stunned now by the stern works of that axe-staff
    to hand.
      Gawain was glad to begin those games in the hall,   495
      For the year's end is now heavy, so have little wonder;
And while men's minds are merry when they have been drinking,
A year winds its full term and rarely it yields
The form at its finish it was sent to unfold.
So this yuletide passed by and the year that did follow,   500
And each season in sequence sued one after other:
Thus after Christmas comes contrary Lent,
Which tries the flesh with the fish and more simple food;
But then the weather of the world with winter it threaps,
Cold clings to the ground, clouds lift up,   505
The rain is shed shining in showers full warm
To fall on the fair fields, and flowers show there,
On the ground and the greensward as though of garments,
Birds bustle to build and brightly do sing
To praise the soft summer which sues thereafter in hill   510
    and bank;
    And blossoms bloom to blow
    By hedgerows richly flanked;
    There's naught so noble now
    As heard in woods so ranked.   515

After the season of summer with its soft winds,
When Zephyrus himself blows on seeds and herbs;
The growth is well joyful that waxes without,
And wet dripping dew drops from the leaves,
Biding full blissful blushes of the bright sun.   520
But then comes high harvest and hardens them soon,
Warning them of the winter so to wax full ripe;
He dries with the drought and makes the dust rise,
From the face of the fields to fly full high;
Wrathful winds in the welkin wrestle with the sun,   525
Leaves loosen from lindens and alight on the ground,
And all grey is the grass that once was so green;
Then all that first rose now ripens and rots,
And thus the year yearns in yesterdays many,
And winter wends again, as the world grows   530
    in age,
  Till Michaelmas moon
  Was come with winter wage.
  Then thinks Gawain full soon
  Of his most anxious voyage.   535

Yet with Arthur he longs through till All Hallows' Day;[†]
And made fair on that feast for that fellow's sake,
With all that rich revelry of the Round Table.
Full courteous knights and comely ladies,
In longing they were for the love of that lord,   540
But nonetheless mentioned nothing but mirth:
Though joyless, they jested for that gentle knight.
Then with mourning, after meat, he mouths to his uncle,
And speaks of his passage and politely he said,
'Now, liege lord of my life, I beg your leave.   545
You know the cause of this case, I need no more
Tell you of its reasons, it would be but trifling;
But I am bound for that blow but barely tomorrow,
To seek that green giant as God wills me wise.'
Then the best of those noblemen busied together,   550
Yvain and Eric with full many others,
Sir Dodinal de Savage, the Duke of Clarence,[†]
Lancelot and Lionel and Lucan the Good,
Sir Bors and Sir Bedevere, big men both,
And Mador de la Port with many other such men.   555
All this courtly company comes near to the king
To counsel this knight with care in their hearts.
In that room the debate was doleful but discreet,
That so worthy as Gawain should wend on that errand,
And endure that dread dent and deal naught by sword's   560
        reply.
    The knight made right good cheer
    And he said, 'What care I?
    Whether fate holds joy or fear,
    What can man do but try?'   565

He dwells there all that day and dresses on the morn,
Asks early for his arms and they were all brought.
First a Toulouse tapestry is laid tight on the floor,
And much was the gilded gear that glinted on top.
That stout man steps on it and he handles the steel,   570
Dubbed in a doublet of the dearest Tharsian,
And then a crafted cap, closed at the top,
That was bordered within with bright bleached blauner.
Then they set the sabatons on that sire's feet,
His legs lapped in steel with lovely greaves   575
And poleyns pitched thereto and polished full clean
About his knees, knitted with knots of gold;
The cuisses then, which cleverly closed
His thick thighs thwart with thongs so attached;
Then a byrnie, embroidered of bright steel rings,   580
Enwrapped in that way upon worthy stuff,
And well-burnished braces upon both his arms,
With good couters gay and gauntlets of plate,
And all the goodly gear to gain him on
     his ride;   585
  With rich coat armour,
  And gold spurs hitched with pride,
  He was girded with a sword full sure
  On a silk belt round his side.

When he was hasped in arms, his harness was rich: 590
Thus even the least loop and lace gleamed of gold.
But harnessed as he was, he still hastens to Mass,
Offered and honoured at the high altar.
Then he comes to the king and to his fellow courtiers,
Taking gracious leave of the lords and the ladies,   595
Then they kissed him and conveyed and commended him to Christ.
By that was Gringolet got ready and girded with a saddle
That gleamed full gaily with many gold fringes,
Everywhere newly nailed and by that note enriched;
The bridle barred about with bright gold binding.   600
The apparel of the peytral and of the proud skirts,
The crupper and caparison accorded with the saddle-bows;[†]
And all was in red, rich-arrayed with gold nails,
Which glinted and glittered as the gleam of the sun.
Then he handles the helmet and kisses it hastily,   605
That was stapled stiffly and stuffed within.[†]
It sat high on his head and was hasped behind,
With a light vrysoun laid over the aventail,
Embroidered and bound with all the best gems
On a broad silken border, and birds on the seams,   610
Such as parrots portrayed amid periwinkles,
Turtle doves and true love blooms, detailed so thick
As if good women about had been stitching seven winters
      in town.
    The circlet was yet more of price   615
    That embraced all his crown –
    Of diamonds, a perfect device
    That glittered bright all round.

Then they showed him the shield that was of sheer gules
With a pentangle picked out in pure gold hues.   620
He bore it by the baldric, arranged about the neck,
Which seemed to that soldier most seemly fair.
And why a pentangle applies to that noble prince
I intend to tell you, though it should tarry me:[†]
It is a sign that Solomon set some while back   625
In betokening of truth, by title that it has,
For it is a figure that holds five points,
And each line interlocks and overlaps with another,
And everywhere it is endless and is in English called
Overall, as I hear, the Endless Knot.[†]   630
This correctly accords to this knight and his arms;
For he is faithful in five ways and in those five again,
Known for his goodness, Gawain was like gold,
Voided of all villainy and with virtue adorned
     by rote.   635
   Therefore, the pentangle new
   He bore in shield and coat,[†]
   Did talk of this lord true
   And the gentlest knight of note.

First he was found faultless in his five senses, 640
Then in his five fingers this fellow never failed,
And all his faith upon earth was in the five wounds
That Christ caught on the cross, as the Creed tells.
And wheresoever this man was stood in a melée,
His first thought was in that, above all other things, 645
That he drew all his fortitude from the five joys
Which the highest queen of heaven had in her child;
And that comely knight had in this cause
Her image depicted in his shield's inner half,
So his courage never failed him when he looked at her. 650
A further five virtues I find in that fellow
Were friendship and fellowship foregoing all things,
His chastity and courtesy beyond reproach,
And pity surpassing all others; these pure five
Were harder hafted to him than to any other. 655
Now truly on this knight were all five times furnished,
And each so harnessed to each other no end could be had,
And fixed upon five points that never failed,
Nor coincided in no side, nor sundered neither,
Without end at any nook I can find anywhere, 660
By tracing my fingers, from beginning to end.[†]
And so on his shining shield thus shaped was that knot
Royally, with rich gold on richer red gules;
Which is the pure pentangle, as called by people
    of lore. 665
  Now got ready is Gawain gay,
  And lays his lance right fore,
  And gives them all good day,
  As he wends for ever more.

He spurred his steed with his spurs and sprung on his way,   670
So swiftly that sparks struck out from the stones.
All those who see him seem sickened at heart,
And said softly the same each one to the other,
Concerned for that knight, 'By Christ, it is shameful
That you, noble lord, shall lose of your life!   675
By faith it is hard to find on this earth such folk.
Surely, to wit, it would have been wiser
To dub yonder dear man a duke as he's earned,
To be in our land a glowing leader of lords,
And so much the better than be broken to naught,   680
So dubbed and beheaded by an elf man for pride!†
Who knew any king to take such counsel
As from knights cavalcading at Christmas games?'
Well much was warm water that wept from their eyes
When that seemly sire swept from those walls   685
     that day.
  He made for no abode
  But brightly went his way;
  Many winding ways he rode
  As I've heard the book does say.†   690

Now rides this knight through the realm of Logres,
Sir Gawain, at God's will, thinking this was no game;
Often friendless, alone, long nights he endures
Where he found naught before him of the fare that he liked.

Now rides this knight through the realm of Logres,
Sir Gawain, at God's will, thinking this was no game.
Often friendless, alone, long nights he endures
Where he found naught before him of the fare that he liked.
He had no friend but his horse through forest and field,   695
Nor no guide as he goes to speak with but God,
Till he neared full nigh into North Wales.
All the isles of Anglesey on his left he beholds,
And he fares over fords between foreshore and foothill,
Crossing at the Holy Head till he found land again   700
In the wilderness of Wirral; few there did live[†]
That loved with good heart either God or great men!
And he sought to find, as he fared, from folk that he met,
If they had heard any talk of a knight all in green,
In any grounds thereabouts, or of the Green Chapel;   705
And all knocked him with a nay, saying never in their lives
Had they seen such a soul that ever was such a hue
    of green.
  The knight took pathways strange
  In many a valley mean;   710
  His cheer often would change
  Before that chapel might be seen.

Many cliffs he climbs over in strange countryside;
And far-flung from his friends as a foreigner he rides.
At each ford that he crossed and waded through water,   715
He found before him a foe, but fabulous it was
That foul though they were, they fell fighting him.
In those mountains our man finds so many marvels
That to tell of one tenth of them would be just tedious!
Sometimes he wars with worms and with wolves,   720
Sometimes with wodwose which dwelled in those crags,
Both with bulls and bears and boars all the while,
And with ogres who harried him in the high fells;
Had he not to our great God with duty been diligent,
He would doubtless be dead and defeated full often.   725
Yet war worried him little for winter was worse,
When the cold, clear water was shed from the clouds,
And falls freezing where it might to the fading earth.
Near slain with the sleet, he slept in his irons
More nights than enough in the naked rocks,   730
Where clattering from the crests came the cold-born rains
And where hung hard icicles high over his head.
Thus, in peril and pain and plights full hard
This knight crossed the country until Christmas Eve
     alone.   735
  And so this knight he cried
  And to Mary did he moan,
  To help him reach and ride
  And guide him to someone.

Sometimes he wars with worms and with wolves,
Sometimes with wodwose which dwelled in those crags,
Both with bulls and bears and boars all the while,
And with ogres who harried him in the high fells.

In the morning he merrily rides by a mountain   740
Full deep into a forest, that was fairly wild
With high cliffs on each half, and wooded holts under
Of full huge hoary oaks, a hundred together;
And the hazel and hawthorn were hunched all the same,
With rough, ragged moss arrayed everywhere,   745
And much baleful were birds on those bare twigs,
That piteously piped there for pain of the cold.
Sir Gawain upon Gringolet glides under them,
Through marsh and through mire, this man all alone,
Concerned for his courtesy lest he not keep his promise   750
To worship our Saviour who on that same night
Was born of a virgin, our burdens to quell.
And thus seeking he said, 'My Lord I beseech you,
And Mary, our mildest mother so dear,
Show me harbour that I might humbly hear Mass   755
And your Matins tomorrow, meekly I ask,
So now priestly I pray my Paternoster, Ave
        and Creed.'
    He rode deep in prayer
    And cried for his misdeeds;   760
    He blessed himself sincere
    And said, 'Christ's cross me speed.'

Now hardly had that knight crossed himself but thrice,
That he saw in that wood a home in a moat,
Above a plain, on a knoll, locked under boughs   765
Of many brawny boles about by the ditches;
The comeliest castle that knight had ever seen,
Perched among pastures, a park all about,
Within a spiked palisade pinned full thick,
That tied in many trees for more than two miles.†   770
Our horseman surveyed that homestead on that side,
As it shimmered and shone through the sheer oaks;
Then he hoists his helm highly and honourably thanks
Jesus and Saint Julian that are both most gracious,
Who had cared for him courteously and heard all his cries.   775
'But I beseech,' said the noble, 'pray grant me good hostelry.'
Then he urges on Gringolet with his gilt heels,
And by good chance he chose to take the chief road,
That brought brightly that noble quick to the drawbridge
        at last.   780
    The bridge was up, not laid,
    The gates were all shut fast,
    The walls were well arrayed;
    That place feared no wind's blast.

The knight bided on his horse and beheld from the bank
Of the deep double ditch that defended that place,
That its walls rose from water wonderfully deep,
And thus a huge height it seemed heaped upon high.

The knight bided on his horse and beheld from the bank   785
Of the deep double ditch that defended that place,†
That its walls rose from water wonderfully deep,
And thus a huge height it seemed heaped upon high
Of hand-hewn stones right up to the corbels,†
In a band under the battlements, in the best manner;   790
And then guard towers full gay all geared between,
With many lovely arrow loops that locked full clean;†
A better barbican that noble had never looked upon.
And within he beheld a hall full high,
All tucked between towers, battlemented full thick,   795
With fine, fair finials all tall and full fixed,
With carved conical caps, craftily skilled.
Many chimneys he chances on, pale as chalk,
Upon bold tower roofs that blinked full white;
So many painted pinnacles were peppered everywhere,   800
Among the castle's crenellations, clustered so thick,
That place purely, it seemed, to be pared out of paper.†
The fine fellow on his horse thought it fair enough,
If he might contrive to come to the cloisters within,
To gain harbour and hostel, while the Holy Day lasted,   805
        so went
    And called, and soon there came
    A porter, true and pleasant,
    Who from that wall asked of his aim
    And greeted the knight errant.   810

'Good sir,' said Gawain, 'would you go on my errand
To the high lord of this house, for me to crave harbour?'
'Yes, by Peter,' said the porter, 'and purely I trust
That you, knight, will be welcome to dwell as you wish.'
Then he went quickly and as swiftly returned,   815
And with other folk freely to favour that knight.
They let down the great drawbridge and dearly went out,
And kneeled down on their knees upon the cold earth
To welcome this warrior as they thought was right;
They greeted him at the broad gate gaping open wide,†   820
And he bid them rise royally and rode over the bridge.
Several souls held his saddle while he alighted,
And sufficient stout men then stabled his steed.
Knights and their squires then all come down
For to bring this noble with bliss to the hall.   825
When he heaved up his helmet high enough, there
They had it from his hand, to serve this high one;
And they took his broadsword and blazoned shield.
Then each one they hailed full highly that horseman,
And many proud men pressed to honour that prince   830
And led him to the hall hasped in his high armour,
Where a fair fire in the hearth fiercely burned.
Then the lord of that land alights from his chamber
To meet with good manners that man on the floor.
He said, 'You are welcome to dwell as you like   835
And treat all here as your own, to wield at your will
        and pace.'
    'Grant mercy,' said Gawain,
    'Let Christ show you his grace.'
    Good fellows they seemed in name   840
    And in their arms they did embrace.

Gawain gazed on the gentleman who greeted him goodly,
And thought what a bold noble that this burgh had;
Indeed, a huge high man and one in his prime.
Broad and bright was his beard and all beaver-hued,   845
Stern, stiff and standing on stalwart shanks,
A face as fierce as fire and free with his speech;
And so fitting it seemed, as our sire truly thought,
That he lead well in lordship hosting other good lords.
That lord chose a side chamber and chiefly commands   850
For a man to deliver Gawain loyal service;
And many men bustled to be bound at his bidding
That brought him to a bright bower, with most noble bedding
Of curtains of clean silk with clear gold hems,
And full curious canopies with fair counterpanes   855
Of bright blauner above and embroidered besides,
With curtains on cords run through red gold rings,
Wall-tight tapestries of Toulouse and Tharsian,
And underfoot, on the floor, fittings to suit.
Then with kind speeches he was disrobed,   860
This baron, of his byrnie and of his bright jupon.
Retainers full rapidly brought him rich robes,
For to check and to change and to choose of the best.
When he had what he wanted and was happy therein
With what sat on him seemly, with sweeping skirts,   865
His visage seemed verily as vibrant as spring
Thought each houseman here, with every hue
Glowing and lovely and covering his limbs,
So that a more comely knight never Christ made,
        they thought.   870
    Whoever in the world he were,
    It seemed as if he ought
    Be a prince without a peer
    In fields where fine men fought.

70

A chair before the chimney, where charcoal burned,   875
Was geared for Sir Gawain, graced well with cloths
And cushions upon quilts which were both well crafted.
And then a merry mantle was cast on that man,
Of a brown blazoned silk, embroidered full rich,
And fair-furred within with fine pelts of the best,   880
All with ermine adorned, his hood of the same.†
And he sat in that settle so seemly rich,
Where warmth charmed him chiefly so that his cheer mended.
Soon a table was touted on trestles full fair,
Clad with a clean cloth that shone a clear white,   885
With some napkins and salt and silvery spoons.
He then washed at his will and went to his meat;
Servants then served him, seemly enough,
With several stews suitable and seasoned well,
Twofold as befalls with many kinds of fish,   890
Some baked in bread, some braised on the coals,
Some simmered, some stewed and savoured with spices,
And all with skilled sauces much to that knight's liking.
The knight called it a feast full freely and often
Full highly, then all that house cheered him at once as   895
            a friend:
    'This penitential fare do take —†
    We'll later make amends!'
    That knight much mirth did make
    As wine in his head did wend!   900

He was then spurred to speak by most sparing questions
Discreetly and privately put to that prince
To learn of him, courteously, from which court he came.
He said it was high Arthur who hailed him as his,
That rich royal king of the Round Table,   905
He said it was Gawain in whose presence they were,
Who had come on his cause that Christmas, as held.
When that lord learned he had this lauded man,
He laughed aloud at it and thought it so likable,
And all the men in that homestead made much joy   910
To appear in the presence so promptly then
Of one whose perfection, prowess and pure manners
Did append to his person and ever were praised;
Who of all mortal men, his repute ranks the most.
Full softly each soul he said to his fellow: 915
'Now shall we see a display of sweet manners
And the spotless techniques of talking so noble;
We shall learn how to speak without speed, unspurred,
Since we have in our fold a fine-nurtured father.
God most truly has given of His grace goodly,   920
That grants us to have such a guest as Gawain,
When blithe nobles of such birth shall sit with us
    and sing!
  Instruction of most manners dear
  This noble shall us bring;   925
  I hope that many men shall hear
  And learn of love-talking.'†

When the dinner was done and the dear ones full up,
It was nigh at the time when the night neared.
Choosing their path, chaplains went to the chapel, 930
Rang bells full richly, right as they should,
For the heavenly evensong of that high season.
The lord takes his leave for it, his lady also;
And they enter most courteously a comely closet.[†]
Gladly, full gay soon Gawain goes there too; 935
Latching him by the sleeve, the lord leads him to sit,
And acquaints with him courteously and calls him his name,
And said he was the most welcome one in the world;
And Gawain thanked him thoroughly and each hailed the other,
Then sat soberly together while that service lasted. 940
Then that lady likes to look on the knight,
So she came from her closet with her charming ladies.
She was the fairest in face, form and looks,
And highest of courtesy, colour and countenance,
And more bewitching than Guinevere, so Gawain thought.[†] 945
As that lady charmed through the chancel to cherish him,
Another lady led her by the left hand,
Who was older than she, an ancient it seemed,
And so highly honoured by that host all about.
But those ladies to look upon were not alike, 950
For if the younger was youthful, the other was yellowed;
Rich red on the one was arrayed everywhere,
While on the other rough wrinkled cheeks rolled;
The kerchiefs of the younger with many clean pearls
Displayed bare her breast and her bright throat, 955
That shone sheerer than snow that is shed on the hills;
That other wore a wimple geared over her neck,
Clinging round her black chin with chalk-white veils,
Her face folded in silk, festooned everywhere,
With tassels all trellised and with trifles about, 960
So naught could be seen but the black of her brows,

Her nose, her naked lips and her two eyes,
Which were sour to see and so strangely bleared;
A model matriarch was she, we may call her†
    by God!   965
  Her body was short and thick
  Her buttocks bulged and broad
  The prettier one to pick
  Was the younger, by accord.

As that lady charmed through the chancel to cherish him,
Another lady led her by the left hand,
Who was older than she, an ancient it seemed,
And so highly honoured by that host all about.

When Gawain glimpsed that lady who looked on him graciously,   970
With leave of the lord, he leant laughing to meet them;
The elder he hails, while bowing full low,[†]
The lovelier in his arms he enfolds a little,
Then kisses her graciously and courteously speaks.
They claim his acquaintance and he quickly asks[†]   975
To be their true servant if they themselves liked.
They take him between them and talking lead him
To a chimneyed chamber and choose quick to ask
For spiced cakes unsparing, which men sped to bring,[†]
At each time of asking with most winsome wine.   980
The lovely lord of that place leaps up and full often,
So many a time minding mirth to be made,
And holding highly his hood hanged it on a spear,
And dared all to win the worship of wearing it
So that most mirth be made at that Christmas time.[†]   985
'And you shall find, by my faith, I will fight at my best
Lest this garment by games I forego to my friends.'
Thus with lots of laughing that lord, he makes merry,
To gladden Sir Gawain with games in the hall
    that night,   990
  Till that time it did arrive
  That the lord he calls for lights,
  And Gawain he did contrive
  To seek his bed for some respite.

On the morning, when each man minds that time   995
When our dear Lord was born, who died for our destiny,
Well-being warms each home in this world for His sake.
So did it there on that day through many delights:
Both at main meal and minor, no matter the size,
Doughty men at that dais did dress of the best.   1000
The old ancient wife, she sits the highest;
The lord sat close loyally, as I understand.
Then Gawain sat together with the gay lady,
Right in the midst where the meal emerged first,
And so through that hall as best seemed to them,   1005
Each guest was served graciously as by their degree.†
There was meat, there was mirth, there was so much joy,
That it would be tiresome for me to tell of it
By attempting to paint it so, peradventure.
Yet I gleaned that Gawain and that gay lady   1010
Did catch together such comfort in company
Through their dear dalliance and discreet talking,
With clean, courteous chatter, free from all sin,
That their pleasure in truth surpassed all princely games
      in there.   1015
   Trumpets and then beating drums
   And piping pleased them fair,
   Each man intent on pleasures won;
   Those two intent on theirs.

Much pleasure was passed that day and the next,   1020
And the third as thoroughly thus thereafter;
The joy of Saint John's Day was glorious to hear,†
Which all the lords knew was the last of the holiday.
The guests were to leave, going in the grey morning,
So they stayed late awake and did drink much wine,   1025
Daintily dancing and carolling dearly.†
At last, when it was late, they begged their leave,
Each to wend on his way, those who did not dwell there.†
When Gawain said goodbye, the good lord he takes him
Unto his own chamber, beside a warm chimney,†   1030
And there draws him close by and dearly he thanks him
For the worshipful wisdom that he had well shown
As to honour his house on that highest tide,†
And embellish his burgh with his beautiful cheer:
'While I live, I would say, sir, that I am worth better   1035
Now that Gawain has been my guest at God's own feast.'
'Gracious thanks, sir,' said Gawain, 'yet in good faith it is yours –
All such honour is your own, may the High King yield you more!†
And I am bound, at your will, to work at your behest
As I am thereto beholden in all matters high and low   · 1040
        by right.'†
    That lord with some great pains
    Tried to detain here that knight,
    But to him answered Gawain
    There was no way that he might.   1045

Then that fellow felt to ask full frankly
What dread deed this Christmas had driven him here
So keenly from Camelot to come all alone,
Before the whole holidays were hailed out of town.
'Indeed, sir,' the knight said, 'you speak but the truth;   1050
A high errand and hasty has brought me from home,
For I am summoned myself to seek such a place,
I know not in this world how to wend so to find.
If by New Year's morn, I have not drawn near it,
So help me our Lord, for all the land in Logres!   1055
So sir, this request I enquire of you here,
That you truly tell me if you ever heard tell
Of the Green Chapel and on which ground it stands,
And of the knight who keeps it, of the colour of green.
We established by statute an assignment between us   1060
To meet at a moot with that man if I might;
And of that ilk the New Year is so nearly upon us,
And I should look on that lord, if God would just let me,
More gladly than on any great wealth, by God's son!
Therefore, sir, by your will, it behoves me to wend,   1065
And be done of my business in just three bare days,
And I would sooner fall flat dead than fail on my errand.'
Then laughing that lord said, 'Now you can stay longer
For I shall take you to that place and in good time.
Getting to the Green Chapel shall grieve you no more;   1070
And you shall sleep in your bed, sir, and at your ease
Pass those days and fare forth on the first of the year,
To make your moot by mid-morn and do as you will in this
     expanse;
   So dwell while New Year's Day   1075
   And rise and rally thence.
   Men shall set you on your way
   For it is barely two miles hence.'

Then Gawain was full glad, and gamely he laughed:
'Now thoroughly I thank you above all other things;   1080
Since near-achieved is my challenge, I shall at your will
Dwell and do so whatsoever you deem.'
Then that noble seized him and beside him he sat,
And let the ladies be fetched for their greater pleasure.
There was much seemly joy by themselves in private;   1085
The lord with delight made loudness so merry
As would seem of his wits that no wits might he have!
Then he spoke to that knight, crying aloud,
'You have deemed so to do any deed that I bid;
Will you hold to your promise right here and at once?'   1090
'Yes, sire, and truthfully,' said his true servant,
'As I bide at your board, I'll be bound by your bidding.'
'You have travelled,' said the lord, 'to us from afar
And stayed wakened with me and are not well refreshed
With sleep nor with sustenance, as I know true.   1095
So you shall long in your lodging and lie at your ease
Till morning and Mass time, then wend to your meal
As you will, with my wife, that shall sit with you
And comfort you with company until I come home at
        the end;   1100
    For early I shall rise
    And on hunting will I wend.'
    Gawain courtly complies,
    Bowing low as knights do bend.

'Yet further,' said the fellow, 'a foreword we shall make: 1105
What I win when in the wood, I will award to you,
And what you chance to achieve you shall exchange with me.
A sweet swap thus between us – swear it now with trust –[†]
Like for like, as it befalls, no matter which is better.'
'By God,' said good Gawain, 'I will grant you this;   1110
And that you like such leisure, well then, I like it too!'
'Who brings us good beer? The bargain is made!'
Said the lord of that place, and then everyone laughed
And they drank and they dallied and debated in trifles,
These lords and ladies, as each of them liked.   1115
Then with French refinement so fair amongst fellows,[†]
They stood still politely while speeches were made,
Courteously kissing, then craving their leave.
Then led lightly by servants with bright glowing torches,
Each noble was brought at the last to his bed,   1120
    most soft:
  To bed, yet more they said,
  Repeating that bargain oft;
  That old lord knew in his head
  How to keep his sport aloft!   1125

FITT 3

Full before daybreak, the folk all arise,
Guests wishing to go did call for their grooms,[†]
And they bustle up briskly, big horses to saddle,
Tightening their tackle, trussing their bags;
The richest dress royally to ride all arrayed,   1130
And leap up lightly, latching their bridles,
Each one going the way that he would like best.
That good lord of this land was not the last
Arrayed for the ride with all of his followers;
He ate a sop hastily, when he had heard Mass,   1135
And with bugling he bustles brisk to the field.
So as first glimpse of daylight gleamed upon earth,
He and his henchmen were on their high horses.
Then those huntsmen with know-how coupled their hounds,
Unlocked the kennel door and called them all out,   1140
Blowing big on their bugles but three bare notes.
Those hounds they bayed back and made fierce barks,
And were chastised and chivvied before they went chasing
By one hundred hunters, as I have heard tell, of
    the best.   1145
   To their trysts dog-keepers go,
   Hounds loosed at their behest;
   And with four good blasts so
   Rose a great row in that forest.

They let the harts through the gate, with their high heads,
The bold bucks also with their broad antler palms;
For the fair lord forbade in close season time
That no man should move so to hunt the male deer.

At the first calls of this quest all the wild game quaked.   1150
Deer drove through the dale, deranged by dread,
Hastening to the heights but heartily they were
Restrained by stout beaters who strongly did shout.[†]
They let the harts through the gate, with their high heads,
The bold bucks also with their broad antler palms;   1155
For the fair lord forbade in close season time
That no man should move so to hunt the male deer.[†]
But the hinds were held in with a 'Hay!' and a 'War!',[†]
The does with a din driven to the deep glades.
There might men see slip the slanting of arrows;   1160
At each wend in the woods as those flights they whistled,[†]
They bit with full broad heads at those big brown beasts.[†]
What! They bray and they bleed in the banks as they die,
And each rushing hound racing readily follows them,
And hunters with high-pitched horns hastening after,   1165
With so cracking a cry as like if the cliffs burst.
What wild ones outwitted all of those shots
Were all rent and raced-out when they were received,[†]
For they were tricked from the hills and teased to the waters;
The lads were so learned at the low trysting places,   1170
And the greyhounds so great at getting there briskly
That they flicked them down as fast as folk might look,
        by right:
    That lord, like blissful boy,
    Would often gallop then alight;   1175
    He drove that day with joy
    And unto the dark of night.

87

Thus the lord is in sport by the edge of a lime wood,
And Gawain the good man lies in his gay bed,
And lurks while the daylight gleamed on the walls,   1180
Under bright-crafted coverlet and curtained about.
And, as from slumbering he slips, slightly he heard
A little din at his door as it opened deftly;
And he heaves up his head just out of the clothes,
A corner of the curtain he casts up a little,   1185
And waits warily there as to what it might be.
It was the lady, loveliest to behold,
That drew the door after her full deftly and still
And bore near to the bed; the noble, ashamed,
Laid himself down lightly and let look like he slept.   1190
And in she stepped silently and stole to his bed,
Cast up the curtain and crept within,
And sat herself softly at the bedside,
And longed there at some length, so to look when he wakened.
The lord lay and lurked, for a long while,†   1195
And composed in his conscience as to what might that case
Amount to or mean − he thought it some marvel −
Yet he said to himself, 'It would be more seemly
To espy with my speech what she wants in this space.'†
Then he wakened and wriggled and turned towards her   1200
And unlocked his eyelids, and looked as in wonder,
And signed himself with the cross by hand; on God he must†
   depend.
  With chin and cheek and smile,
  Which white and red did blend,   1205
  Did she with words beguile
  And small laughing lips befriend.

It was the lady, loveliest to behold,
That drew the door after her full deftly and still
And bore near to the bed; the noble, ashamed,
Laid himself down lightly and let look like he slept.

'Good morning, Sir Gawain,' said that gay lady,
'You are a sleeper unskilled that I may slip here.
You are taken and tied, lest we may shape a truce,   1210
I shall bind you in your bed, that you may believe!'
All laughing the lady, she parleyed through banter.
'Good morning, my gay,' said blithe Gawain,
'I shall work as you will – and that I like well,
For I yield myself readily and cry for your mercy;   1215
And I deem that is best because I am bound.'
And thus he bantered again with much blithe laughter.
'But would you, lovely lady, then grant me leave,
And unpress your prisoner and pray him to rise,†
So to be off this bed better dressed to be with you;   1220
And catch me more comfort so then to speak?'
'No, truly, fair sir,' said she so sweet,
'You must remain in your bed, it is for me better
To hasp you in here, your other half also,†
And then speak with my knight that I have caught here.   1225
Then I would well know you are truly Gawain,
Who all the world worships wherever you ride;
And whose honour and handiwork is all highly praised
By lords, by ladies and by all that live here.
And now you are here, we are truly alone;   1230
My lord and his lads do fare long away,
Other nobles be in bed and my ladies also,
The door is drawn doubly, shut with a stout hasp;
And since I have in this house he who all like,
I shall wend my time well, while it lasts, with   1235
        talk-tale.
    You are welcome to my form
    To do with as you entail;
    Duty bound I shall perform
    As your servant without fail.'   1240

90

'In good faith,' said Gawain, 'I think this agreeable,
Though I do not know of he that you speak;
To reach heights of such reverence as you relate here,
I am not worthy, I would well know myself.
By God, if you thought it good, I would be glad   1245
Just merely to serve you as you would see fit,
At your pleasure and price – it would be a pure joy.'
'In good faith, Sir Gawain,' said the gay lady,
'With your praised name and prowess that pleases all others,
Not to love you like they do would make me discourteous.   1250
There are so many ladies alive now that would
Have you highly in their hold as I have you here,
To dally with dearly on your dainty words,
Catching of comfort and cooling their cares,
That they'd give of their guarded gold all that they had.   1255
But I laud our dear Lord that rules all of high heaven,
That I have in my hands all that others desire,
    Through grace!'
  She made him of such great cheer,
  That was so fair of face;   1260
  And the knight with speeches clear
  Answered well without disgrace.

'Madam,' said the merry man, 'may Mary grant you much,
For in good faith I have found you most noble and generous;
The fine company of others can finesse many fellows,   1265
But I do not deserve deference dealt to me –
It is the worship of you which brings only good.'
'By Mary,' said that mistress, 'methinks it otherwise;
Were I the equal in worth to all women alive,
And all the wealth of the world were in my hand,   1270
And I should chivvy and chance to choose me a man,
For the quality I know and see before me sir knight,
Of the beauty and courtesy and blithe resemblance,
That I have seen here and can hold to be true,
Then no finer fellow would I choose before you.'   1275
'Well, my worthy,' said the knight, 'you have chosen one better;†
But I am proud of the price that you place on me
And soberly, as your servant, I hold you my sovereign,
And your knight I become, and may Christ reward you!'
Thus they sweet-mouthed of much-what till mid-morning passed,   1280
And long the lady let like she loved him greatly;
The knight, he was faithful and acted full fair.
Though no brighter beauty had that noble known,
Love lessened in his looks as he thought of life's loss
      to come;   1285
  The blow that should him cleave,
  As needs it must be done.
  The lady sought her leave
  Which he granted her as won.

Then she gave him good day and glanced at him, laughing,   1290
And as she stood, she stunned him with these strong words:
'Now may He who speeds speech help you with what follows;
For that you be Gawain goes not in my mind.'
'Wherefore?' said our fellow, and freshly he asks,
Afraid of some failure in the form of his manners.   1295
But that beauty, she blessed him and said 'For this reason:
If Gawain is so good as is gamely beheld,
Who clasps all his courtesy clean to himself,
He would not have lingered so long with a lady
And yet not crave a kiss by his courtly manners,   1300
With some hint or some trifle to sum up his talk.'
Then said Gawain, 'I would do as you wish;
At your command, I shall kiss you, as should a knight
Lest he displease you, so plead it no more.'
With that she comes near and clasps him in her arms,   1305
Lowers down lovingly and kisses the lord.
Then they comely commend each other to Christ;†
She departs by the door with no more discussion,
So he reaches to rise and quickly he rushes,
Calls to his chamberlain, chooses his clothes   1310
And bustles forth when he was robed, blithely to Mass.
Then he moved to his meal, which was made in his honour,
And then made merry all day, till the moon rose,
    with games.
  No knight fared better than among   1315
  These two dignified dames,
  The older lady and the young;
  Much joy each gave the same.

And the lord of that land, he relaxes in sport,
Hunting in holt and heath for hornless hinds.   1320
Such a sum he slayed there by when the sun set,
Of does and other deer, it were wondrous to deem.
Then at the last, the folk fiercely flocked in
And quickly a quarry of killed deer they made.
The best men bristled forth with enough of their boys,   1325
Gathered the greatest in fat that there were,†
And did dearly undo them, as so the deed asks:
They sized them at the assay, those men that were skilled,
And found just two fingers of fat on the feeblest!
Then they slit the breast slots and they seized at the erber,   1330
Shaved it free with a sharp knife and knotted the tripes.
Next they ripped off the four limbs and rent the hide,
Then they break the belly and they took out the bowels
Lightly, lest they did loosen their knot.
They gripped at the gullet and gravely departed   1335
The throat from the windpipe and whipped out the guts.
Then they slit out the shoulder joints with their sharp knives,
Hooked out through a little hole to keep those sides whole.†
Then they made the breast brittle and broke it in two,
And again at the gullet they then begin,†   1340
Readily ripping it, right to the branch,
Voiding it of offal and verily thereafter
All the membranes by the ribs, they loosen readily.
And so by this ritual, rid it to the ridge bones,
Right up to the haunches so it hanged all the same,   1345
And heaved it up all whole and hewed it off there –
And all this they name the numbles, as I know it to be true
           by kind.†
       By the branching of the thighs
       They loosen flaps behind;   1350
       Hewing quick in two as wise,
       By the spine those deer were chined.†

Both the head and the heavy neck they hew off then,
And then they sundered the sides, swift from the chine,
And the fee for the raven they cast in a grove.†   1355
Then they pierced either thick side, through by the ribs,†
And both then they hanged by the hocks of the haunches,
Each fellow paid his fee in flesh as is due.†
Upon the hide of that fine beast, they fed their hounds†
With the liver and the lungs and the leather of their paunches†   1360
And bread bathed in blood blended like stew.
They blew bold for the kill and loud bayed their hounds,
Then they took that fine flesh and then fared for home,
Striking horns full stoutly with many strong notes.
Thus when daylight was done those doughty did win   1365
Into that comely castle where our knight bides
    full still,
  With bliss and bright fire set.
  The lord, he came there till
  With Sir Gawain was he then met,   1370
  And both talked with joy at will.

Then that sire in his hall summoned all by sure command,
And both ladies also to alight with their maids.
Before all the folk, his fellows he bids
To fetch all his venison verily before him;   1375
And all gamely he also called good Sir Gawain,
Teaches him the full tale of each well-caught beast,
And shows him the shining grease, shimmering on ribs.
'Does this sport please you? Have I won a prize?
Am I thanked thoroughly through my craft so served?'   1380
'Why, yes,' said that other one, 'these are the best winnings
That I have seen in the winter these last seven years.'
'All this I give you, Gawain,' said that good man,
'By accord of our covenant it is yours to claim.'
'This is so,' said the knight, 'and I say to you likewise: 1385
That which I won worthily within this, your dwelling,
I likewise with goodwill give it to you.'
He hasps his fair neck heartily in his arms,
And kisses him courteously, as best as he could:
'Take this my achievement, I chanced on no more;   1390
I vouchsafe it full fairly, just as if it were finer.'
'It is good,' said the great lord, 'many thanks I grant you.
Maybe your prize is better – perhaps you could brief me
Where you won this sweet wealth by the strength of your wits?'
'That was not in our foreword,' he said, 'do play fairly;†   1395
For you have taken of your terms, and so truly cannot
        have more.'
    They laughed and they made blithe
    With talking and uproar;
    And when the meal arrived   1400
    There were dainties by the score.

And so by the chimney they sat in a chamber,
With men by the wall wielding wine to them often,[†]
And often bold did they boisterously bid in the morning
To fulfil the same foreword they had made before: 1405
That as chance so betides to exchange their achievements,
What new things they gained when they met the next night.
They accorded that covenant before all that court –
With beverages brought forth to seal this bargain –
Then they lovingly took their leave at the last   1410
And each man bounded briskly up to his bed.
By the time the cock crowed and cackled but thrice,
The lord leapt from his bed, his followers also,
And their meat and their Mass was metely completed,
And they drove to those woods, before the day dawned, to   1415
  the chase.
 High with hunt and horns,
 Through plains they pass in space,
 Released among those thorns,
 Those hounds they ran a race!   1420

Then they beat on the bushes and bade him rise up,
And then suddenly, swiftly he escaped those hunters;
The most stunning swine that ever sprang out,
Long since from the sounder, single and separate.

Soon, dogs scent their quarry and cry out by a quagmire;
Hailing hunters urged those hounds who first noticed it,
And wild words they bellow with a worthy noise.
Those hounds that heard it hastened there swiftly,
And fell fast to the footprints, forty at once.   1425
Then the gushing and gambolling of those gathered hounds
Rose such that the rocks there rung all about;
Hunters all heartening them with horn and mouth.†
Then all as assembled swayed together
Between a flood in that forest and a fierce crag.   1430
In a knot, by a cliff, at the quag-side,
There as the rough rocks raggedly had fallen,
They fared to their find, with fellows thereafter.
They cast about crags and the dark thickets both,
Until they were wise as to where was within them   1435
The beast and the object of their bloodhounds.
Then they beat on the bushes and bade him rise up,
And then suddenly, swiftly he escaped those hunters;
The most stunning swine that ever sprang out,
Long since from the sounder, single and separate,†   1440
He was brimming and bold, a boar amongst boars,
Full grim when he grunted; then many grieved,
When at the first thrust he threw three men to earth
And spurred forth at good speed without more respite.
Men hailed, 'Hi!' loudly and cried, 'Hey – hey!'   1445
Holding horns to their lips as they herded the pack;
Many was the merry mouth of those men and hounds
That bound after this boar with boasting and noise
        to quell.
    Full often he turns at bay   1450
    And maims those dogs full well;
    He hurts those hounds and they
    Full sadly yowl and yell.

Sharp bowmen shoved forth to shoot at him then,
And let hail their arrows, hitting him often;   1455
But those pricking points just jumped off his shoulders,
And of his brow those barbs would bite not one bit,
As their shaven shafts shattered in pieces
And the arrow heads hopped off wherever they hit.[†]
But when these dents did him damage from their drubbing strokes,   1460
Then, brain-raged for bait, on those bowmen he rushes,
Hurts them full heartily from where he hails forth,
And so many, afraid, they fleetly drew back.
But the lord on a light horse launches after him,
And bent upon boldness his bugle he blows;   1465
He rallied and rode through bushes full thick,
Pursuing this wild swine till the sun set.
So in this way on that day did they drive on this deed,
While our lovely lord, he lies in his bed,
Gawain most gracious at home in gear full rich   1470
     of hue.
  The lady did not forget
  To greet Gawain anew;
  Full early off she set
  To try to change his view.   1475

She comes to the curtain and peeps at the knight.
Sir Gawain, he welcomed her worthily at once,
And she gives him again the full joy of her words,
Sits softly by his side and sweetly she laughs,
And with lovely looks she let sing of these words: 1480
'Sir, if indeed you are Gawain, I wonder and think,
Why a warrior so worthy and in all ways so good,
Knows nothing of courtliness nor of its customs,
And when folk give you knowledge you cast it away;
For you have quickly forgot what I taught yesterday   1485
By token of the truest of talk that I know.'
'What's that?' said Gawain, 'I would never do that;
If it be as you brief, then the blame is all mine!'
'Yet I schooled you in kissing,' said that comely one,
'And where such customs are cultured, then be quick to claim,   1490
As becomes such a knight who calls himself courteous!'
'Do away with such speech, my dear,' said Gawain,
'For I dare not do that lest I were denied;
And if proffered then refused, I would wit I was wrong.'
'By my faith,' said the merry wife, 'who would refuse you;   1495
Who has stout strength enough to constrain as you wish
Any who were so villainous as would deny you?'
'Well, by God,' said Gawain, 'your speaking is good,
But threats are ill-thought of in the land where I live,
As are gifts that are given when not made with goodwill.   1500
I am at your command to kiss when you like;
You may learn what you like and leave off as you think is
    the case.'
   The lady bows low down
   And does sweetly kiss his face;   1505
   With much speech they then expound
   Of love's agony and its grace.

'I would wish to learn of you,' that worthy she said,
'If you were not wrathful, what would be the reason†
That so young and so youthful as you at this time,   1510
So courteous, so knightly, as you are known widely –
And in the chronicles of chivalry the chief thing most praised
Is the loyal lore of love, its letters of arms;†
For it tells in such teaching of the truest of knights,
In the title and token and text of its works,†   1515
How for pure love's sake ventured lords for their ladies,
Endured for their doting the most dreadful of days,
Avenged with their valour and avoided all care
And brought bounteous bliss to the bowers of their ladies –†
And you are acclaimed the most courteous known knight,   1520
Whose word and whose worship walks far and wide,
And has sat by yourself with me two different times,
Yet I never heard your head herald those words
That ever spoke love at much length or a little!
For you, who are courteous and crafted in manners,   1525
Ought to a young one be yearning to show
And teach some tokens of true love's crafts!
Why! Are you low-witted, despite your renown,
Or else deem me too dim to behold of your dalliance?
     For shame!   1530
   I come here alone and sit
   To learn from you love's game.
   Do teach me of your wit,
   While my lord elsewhere seeks fame.'

'In good faith,' said Gawain, 'may God yield you wealth!   1535
It brings me great glee and also huge joy
That so worthy as you would wind up here,
And pain you with so poor a man to play with as your knight
With all kinds of compliance; it comforts me greatly!
But to trouble myself to expound on true love,   1540
And teach of the themes, texts and tales of chivalry
To you who, I know well, has far more skill
In that art, by half, of a hundred of me
As I am now or ever shall be, so long as I live on earth,
It would be folly full-fold, fair lady, in truth.   1545
But I would at your willing, work with my might,
As I am highly beheld, and evermore will
Be a servant to you, so save me dear God.'
Thus this fair lady fished and often tried to find out,
How to win him great woe by what means that she could;   1550
But his defence was so fair no offence could be made,
Nor no evil, by neither half; naught could be wrought
     but bliss.
   They laughed and talked for long;
   She at last gave him a kiss,   1555
   Then speaking sweet with tongue
   She went her way with this.

Then our warrior, he stirs and rises for Mass,
And then their dinner was ready and dearly served.
Thus that lord with the ladies relaxed all day,   1560
But the lord of these lands launched out full often,
Seeking that ugly swine that swings through the banks,
Which bit his best hounds their backs asunder,
Then did bide at full bay till the bowmen did out it
By maddening his mind to make him come forth.   1565
Yet though flights of arrows fell when those folk gathered,
He made them astounded being stubborn to startle,
But at last he was so spent he might run no more,
And with what haste he can muster, he wins to a hole
In a rise, by a rock, where runs the bourn.   1570
He gets the bank at his back, and begins to scrape,
The froth foamed in his mouth, foul at the corners,
As he whets his white tusks. With him so irked
All the boys so bold stood back from him, so
To harm him from afar, for none dares come nearer   1575
    for woe:
  He had hurt so many before
  That all there were so loathe
  To be by his tusks torn,
  Who was fierce and bad-brained both.   1580

Till the knight comes himself, coaching his horse,
And sees that boar at abeyance beside all his men.
He alights lovingly and leaves his courser,
Brings out a bright blade, and bigly strides forth,[†]
Forcing fast through the ford where that fierce one bides.   1585
The wild boar was wary of that one with the weapon,
His hackles rose high and so huffily he snorted
That folk feared for their fellow lest he fared the worse.
The swine sets out straight at that lord, so
That both noble and boar bundled all in a heap   1590
In the whiteness of the water; that other was worse off
For the man marked him well, as they first met,
And set stoutly that sword pushing into his throat,
So right up to its hilt that it shattered his heart,
And growling he gave, gulped by the waters   1595
        full tight.
    A hundred hounds did grab that boar
    With fierceness in their bite.
    Men dragged him to the shore
    And of his death those dogs made light.   1600

There was a blowing at the prize of many a bright horn,
High halloos and higher shouted mightily by men;
Hounds bayed for that beast as bid by the masters
Of that charging chase who were the chief huntsmen.
Then a man wise in the ways of such woodcrafts   1605
Lovingly begins to unlace this boar.
First he hacks off his head and sets it on high,
And thereafter rents him all rough by the ridge,
Draws out the bowels and broils them on brands,
With bread blended therewith, rewarding the hounds.   1610
Then he cuts out the brawn in bright broad slices,
And he has out the entrails as highly beseems;
Then he hitches together the halves all whole,
And then on a stiff staff he hangs them stoutly.
Now with this swine they swing then to home   1615
With the head of that boar borne before that great noble
Who had felled him in the foam through force of his hand
    so strong.
  In the hall he sees Gawain
  After that day so long;   1620
  He called him and he came
  For his dues before the throng.

The lord, full merry, laughed aloud much
When he sees Sir Gawain and with joyfulness speaks.
The good ladies were gathered, as was the great court;   1625
He shows them the meat sides, and shares them the tale
Of the largeness, the length and the lividness also
Of the war of the wild swine in the wood where he fled.
That other knight courteously commended his deeds,
And praised this great prize as proof of his skill,   1630
For such brawn from a beast, the bold noble said,
Nor such sides of a swine has he ever seen.
Then they handled the huge head; our high knight, he praised it
And loudly did laud it so to honour that lord.
'Now, Gawain,' said the good man, 'this gain is your own   1635
By our fastened foreword, so faithfully accorded.'
'It is so,' said the knight, 'and assuredly true,
All that which I won I shall give you again as agreed.'
He clasped the lord by the neck and kisses him courteously,
And again of the same one more he served there.†   1640
'Now we are,' said Gawain, 'in this eventide even
Of every covenant we knit since I came here and did
     avow.'
  The lord said, 'By Saint Giles
  You are the best man that I know!   1645
  You'll be rich in a short while
  With such winnings that you grow.'

Then they took tables and set them on trestles,
With cloths to cover them; then many clear lights
And waxen torches did awaken the walls; 1650
Thus servants set supper in that hall all around.
Much glamour and glee glistened in there
About the fire on that fine hearth and they fell again
At the supper and after; many noble songs,
And much new carolling, did conjure of Christmas 1655
With all the mannerly mirth that man may tell of.
While as always our lovely knight sat by the lady;
Such seemly sweetness did she make to him,[†]
With soft stolen looks to please that stalwart,
That he was dumbfounded, and he was worried, 1660
But he would not by his learning return her advances,
And dealt with her daintily howsoever his deeds might
    be cast.
  When they had played in that hall
  As long as they could last, 1665
  That lord did Gawain call,
  And to a fireplace they passed.

And there they drank and they dallied and deemed often anew
To renew of their covenant on New Year's Eve.
But the knight craved leave to decamp in the morning,   1670
For it was nigh at the term to which he had been tied.
But the lord yearned for him to stay longer awhile
And said, 'I grant you my word as the truest of lords,
You shall achieve the Green Chapel as you are so charged,
By first light of New Year, lord, and long before prime.   1675
Therefore lie in your loft and relax at your ease,
And I shall hunt in this holt and hold to our handshake,
Exchanging achievements as we are so charged;
For I have twice fashioned tasks and both times found you faithful.
Now, third time throws best! Think on in the morning;   1680
Let's make merry while we may, and mind ourselves upon joy,
Our life is for living – we can mope at our leisure!'
This was agreed eagerly, Sir Gawain he would stay,
Then drink was brought blithely and they went to bed by
    torch bright.   1685
  Sir Gawain lies and sleeps
  Full still and soft all night;
  The lord who his scheme keeps
  Arose early at first light.

After Mass he took morsels along with his men;   1690
Most fine was the morning, and he asks for his mount.
All the host on their horses who would follow him
Were all bridled and bustling before the hall gates.
Fine fair were those fields for there the frost clung;
And in red on ruddied rack rises the sun   1695
And coasts full clear in the clouds of the welkin.
Hunters unharnessed hounds at a holt-side,†
Rocks rang from the racket that rose from their horns.
Sniffing, some hounds fall on a fox scent,
Criss-crossing in trails by the trait of their ways.   1700
A whippet cries out and calls the pack to him;
His fellows all follow him, frothing full thick,
Running forth in a rabble, right hard where he fared.
Where that fox flies before them, they found him quite soon,
And they swiftly pursued him when he was in sight,   1705
Whipping him wilfully with their wrathful noise;
And he tricks and he turns through many a tight thicket,
As he halts and harkens by hedges full often.†
Till at last, by a little ditch, he leaps over a hurdle,
Steals out full still by a slough strand,   1710
And went out of those woods to outwit those hounds.
But he then, unawares, wandered well near a tryst,
Where three throaty hounds threatened him at once,
        all grey;
    He blanched again with strife   1715
    And stiffly starts at bay,
    With all the woe in life
    To the wood he shot away.

Full often he was run at wherever he arose
And often ran back also, so wily was Raynard.
And that lord and his men he led them by the heels,
In this manner, by those mountains, while mid over noon.

Then it lifted all life to listen to these hounds,
When all that mob came upon him and mingled together!   1720
Their sight put such sorrow in the head of that fox,
Like the clambering cliffs had clattered on him in heaps.
Here was he hallooed when he met with the huntsmen,
Loud was he greeted with their growling speech;
There was he threatened and often called 'thief'.   1725
With all the terriers at his tail, he dared never tarry;
Full often he was run at wherever he arose
And often ran back also, so wily was Raynard.
And that lord and his men he led them by the heels,
In this manner, by those mountains, while mid over noon,   1730
While our high knight at home, he wholesomely sleeps
Within comely curtains on that cold morning.
But that lady, for love, lies not at sleep,
Nor the purpose be parried that pitched in her heart,
But up she rose readily and rushed her there   1735
In a merry mantle which met to the earth,
That was fully furred with fine pelts all well pared,
No headdress on her head, save for higher gemstones
Traced round her tresses in clusters of twenty;†
Her thriving face and her throat thrown all naked,   1740
Her breast bare before and also behind.†
She comes in by the chamber door and closes it after,
Waves up a window and calls on Gawain,†
And thus readily rallied him with her rich words
     and cheer: 1745
  'Ah, man, how may you sleep?
  This morning is so clear!'
  He was in drowsing deep
  But then he heard her here.

In dream-devilled drowsing drabbled that noble,   1750
As a man so brought to mourning by many troubled thoughts
Of how destiny should that day deal him his fate
At the Green Chapel when he meets the Green Knight,
And bides his blow as is bid, without further debate.
But when that comely she came, he recovered his wits,   1755
He swings out of his slumbers and answers with haste.
That lovely lady came laughing so sweet,
And fell about his fair face and fondly kissed him;
He welcomes her worthily with a warm cheer.
He sees her so glorious and gaily attired,   1760
So faultless of her features and of such fine complexion,
That with welling joy she warmed his heart.
With smooth smiling soft, they submitted to mirth,
Such that all was bliss and bonchief that between them broke
      so fine.   1765
   They uttered words so good,
   Much joy there was entwined;
   Yet great peril between them stood
   Should Mary not her knight so mind.†

For that priceless princess pressed him so thick,   1770
Nudged him so near to breaking that he felt needs must
Either latch to her love or so rudely refuse.
Yet he cared for his courtesy, lest he seemed a scoundrel,
And much more so for his plight, if he should commit sin
And betray that dear lord in whose tower he lodged.   1775
'God shield me,' said the knight, 'that I shall not fall!'
With a little love-laughing he deflected aside
All those speeches so special that sprung from her mouth.
To that noble the lady said, 'Blame you deserve
If you love not that life which lies next to you,   1780
Of all women in this world the most wounded in heart,
Unless you have a lady you love and like better,
And are freely pledged faithful to her and hard-fastened
So you'll not loosen lightly, that's what I believe!
Thus give me the facts frankly now, please, I pray you;   1785
For all the love that gives life do not silence the truth
    by guile.'
  The knight said, 'By Saint John,'
  And smoothly with a smile,
  'In faith I have right none –   1790
  Nor none do I want the while.'

'That is a word,' said the woman, 'that is worst of all;
But I am so answered, and that in truth makes me sad.
Kiss me now knight and I shall clear from here;
Long to mourn in this realm as made low by much love.'[†]   1795
Sighing, she sways down and seemly kissed him,
And then severs from him and says as she stands,
'Now, dear one, at this departing, please do me this pleasure:
Give me as a gift somewhat of yourself, if only your glove,
That I may think of you, man, to lessen my mourning.'   1800
'Now I wish,' said our worthy, 'I would I had here
The best thing in this land that I wield for your love,
For you have truly deserved so astoundingly often
More reward, I might reason, than I could reach for.
But to deliver for doting so little a dainty?!   1805
It would deal you dishonour to have at this time
A mere glove as a gesture of Gawain's gift,
For I am here on an errand in earths unknown,
And have no men with hampers of marvellous things;[†]
And I dislike this, my lady, for love at this time,   1810
But a man so taken must do as he's took, so do not ill
          or pine.'
     'No, no, man of high honours,'
     Said that lovely dressed fine,
     'Though I have naught of yours,   1815
     Yet you shall have of mine.'

She offered him a rich ring of red-golden work,
With a stone like a star, standing aloft,
That blushed there and beamed just like the bright sun;
Mark you well, it was worth a great wealth full huge.   1820
But the warrior refused it and readily he said:
'By God, I wish no gifts, my gay, at this time;
I can give none in return, so naught will I take.'
She bade it him busily but he waives her bidding,
And truly swears swiftly he would not receive it;   1825
And forsaken with sorrow, she then said thereafter,
'If you refuse my ring for seeming too rich,
And would not be so highly beholden to me,
I shall give you my girdle, a gain of less value.'
A belt she loosed lightly that was locked round her sides,   1830
Knit round her gown, underneath the bright mantle,
It was geared with green silk and trimmed with gold,
Bestitched and embroidered by hand all around;
This she gave the noble and blithely she begged
That though it seemed worthless, she hoped he would take it.   1835
And yet he said no, he would never in no way
Neither gold nor no gift take till God sent his grace
To achieve of the challenge he had chosen there.
'And therefore, I pray you, be not displeased,
And let be your business, for I cannot consent to   1840
          your grant.
     I am ever in your debt, be told,
     And for your kindness want,
     Whether it is hot or cold,
     To be your true servant.'   1845

'Do you forsake this silk,' said that lady then,
'Because it is too simple, as so it might seem?
Ah! Yes, it is little but no less is it worthy.
For whoso knew the comforts that are knit therein,
I think would appraise as more prized peradventure;   1850
For what good knight is so girt with this green lace,
While he has it closely hitched all about him,
There is no mortal man that might hew him down,
For by no scheme on earth might this man be slain.'
Then that knight considered and he came to think   1855
For the jeopardy ahead that he judged it a jewel:†
When he achieved the Green Chapel to fetch him his blow,
If he escaped unslain, the sleight would be noble!
Then swayed by her words, he suffered her to speak
And she bore the belt on him and urged him to bear it –   1860
And he granted her wish, giving in with goodwill –
And besought him, for her sake, never to disclose it,
Nor let her lord know it; the knight, he accords
That he would tell no one and only those two would
      know aught.   1865
   He thanked her often and full swift
   From his heart and with thought.
   By that, on three sides – gifts –
   She then kissed that knight so taut.

Then she takes her leave and she leaves him there,   1870
For she could not get more amusement from him.
When she was gone Gawain swiftly gets ready,
Rises and attires in rich noble array,
Folds up the love-lace that lady gave him,
And full wholly he hid it securely for later.   1875
Then chiefly he chooses the way to the chapel,
Approached a priest there for a private confession,
So to learn how to live his life more for the better
That his soul should be saved when he should see heaven.
There, sheer he was shrived and showed his misdeeds,   1880
Both the major and minor, and mercy he begs,
And for absolution he asks of that priest;
And he surely absolved him and set him so clean,
To be ready for Doomsday if so dealt on the morn.†
Then he makes himself merry among the free ladies,   1885
With most courtly carolling and all kinds of joy,
As he had not done till that day, and to the dark night,
     with bliss.
  All were delighted there
  With him and said, 'He is   1890
  So much happier and more fair
  Since he first came here to this.'

Now let him long there and let love embrace him!
Still out on the land the lord leads his men.
He has flushed out the fox that he has long followed;   1895
    As he sprung through a spinney to espy that rascal,
    There he hears those hounds that harassed him swiftly,
And Raynard comes rushing fast through some rough growth,
With all that rabble in a race and right at his heels.
The lord saw that wild one and warily moves back,   1900
And brings out his bright sword and strikes at the beast.
And he shied from that sharp blade and should have shrunk back;
But a greyhound rushed on him before he might do so,
And before the great feet of the horse they fell on him
And worried that wily one loudly with wrath.   1905
The lord alights brightly and, lifting him swiftly,
Raised that fox readily out of their red mouths,
Holds it high over his head, and fast halloos,
And many brave hounds all bayed at him there.
Then huntsmen hurried there with many loud horns,   1910
And they rallied as was proper till they saw their lord.
And by that then his noble company gathered,
All that ever bore bugles blew them at once,
And those others that had no horns they all hallooed;
No merrier music had men ever heard,   1915
This rich racket so raised there for Raynard's soul
        by rote;
    Their hounds they did reward,
    And fondled heads and throats,
    And then they took Raynard   1920
    And tore off all his coat.

And then they headed for home for it was nigh upon night,
Striking full stoutly on their stern horns.
At last at his loved home, the lord then alights,
Finds the fire on the hearth, our fellow beside it,   1925
Sir Gawain the good, contented and glad,
Among those lovely ladies where he learned much joy.
He wore a blue tunic that flowed broad back to the ground;
His surcoat well seemed him for it was soft furred,
And his hood of the same it hung on his shoulder,   1930
With both trimmed about with a band of blauner.
He meets that good man in the midst of the floor,
And with grace he greeted him and gaily said,
'This time I'll be first to fulfil our foreword,
When we spoke speedily and no drink was spared.'   1935
He embraces the lord and he kisses him thrice,
As sufficient and sweetly as he should be able.†
'By Christ,' said that other knight, 'you catch much fortune
In achieving those winnings if you chanced them cheaply.'
'Yes, no charge and by choice!' said that other chiefly,   1940
'As I openly paid the price that I ought.'†
'My,' said that other man, 'mine is the lesser
For I have hunted all day and I have got naught
But this foul fox fur – the Fiend take these goods! –†
And that is payment full poor for such princely things   1945
As you have thrust on me thoroughly in these three kisses
        so good.'
    'Enough,' said Sir Gawain,
    'I thank you, by the rood.'
    And how that fox was slain   1950
    He then learned of as they stood.

With mirth and with minstrelsy and meats of their choice,
They made as merry as any men might –
With laughing of ladies and with lots of banter,
Gawain and the good man they both seemed so glad –   1955
That in dotage or drunken all those lords did appear.
Both these men and the household made many japes,
Till the hour, it was come when sleep came to summon
Those nobles to bed as by rights they did go.
Bowing low, Sir Gawain first takes leave of the lord   1960
And favours that noble with fine and fair thanks:
'For such splendid sojourn as I have had here,
Your high feast and your hosting, may the High King reward you!
I'll pledge you my service for one of your own, if you will,
For I must, as you know, make to move on the morrow,   1965
And take some tutor to teach me, as you have promised,
The way to the Green Chapel, as great God wills me suffer
To be dealt on New Year's Day the doom I have earned.'
'In good faith,' said the good man, 'with a goodwill;
All that which I promised you, I will fulfil.'   1970
He assigns him a servant to show him the right way
And lead him through the downs so he would not delay,
And fare fast through the forest by the shortest path
      that weaves.
   The Lord Gawain then said his thanks   1975
   For what he had received;
   Of those ladies high in rank
   The knight then took his leave.

With care and with kissing, he speaks with them now,
And with heartfelt feeling he thoroughly thanks them,   1980
And promptly likewise they praised him in reply,
And to Christ they commended him with downcast sighs.
Then from them all he departs with good manners;
Each man that he met, he mindfully thanks
For his service, society and his several pains   1985
That had been his business and boon to supply;
And each soul was as sorry to sever with him there
As if they had always lived with that worthy one.
Then with loyally held lights, he was led to his chamber
And brought blithely to bed to be at his rest.   1990
If he sleeps not soundly, I dare not say,
For he had much on the morning to mind, if he would,
      in thought.
    Let him lie there still,
    He is near what he has sought;   1995
    And if you will a while be still,
    I will tell you how things wrought.

FITT 4

Now nears the New Year and the night passes,
The dawn drives back the dark as the Lord commands.
But wild winter storms out there were awake;   2000
Clouds cast the cold keenly to earth,
With nigh enough of the north to tan naked skin.
The stinging snow showers snapped at the wildlife;
The whistling winds whipped from the heights,
And drove each dale full of great deep drifts.   2005
Our lord listened full well, that lies in his bed,
Though he locks his lids, he sleeps but little;
By each cock that crowed he knew well his fate neared.
Speedily he got dressed before that day dawned,
For there was light from a lamp that glowed in his chamber.   2010
He called to his servant, who answered him quickly,
And bade him bring his byrnie and his bold saddle;
That other goes fast and fetches his garments,
And in a great way he gets Sir Gawain ready.
First he clad him in clothes to keep him from the cold,   2015
Then the rest of his things that had been kept with care,
Both his paunce and his plates, picked full clean,
And the rich rings of his byrnie, rattled of their rust;[†]
And all was fresh as it first was, so he offered warm thanks
          of course.   2020
     He put on every piece,
     Wiped clean with great resource –
     The finest man from here to Greece;[†]
     The knight bade bring his horse.

But wild winter storms out there were awake;
Clouds cast the cold keenly to earth,
With nigh enough of the north to tan naked skin.
The stinging snow showers snapped at the wildlife.

As he wrapped himself up in his most noble clothing –   2025
His surcoat and badge speaking of cleanest virtue,
Emblazoned on velvet with virtuous stones
All beaten and bound in embroidered seams,
And fair-furred within with the finest of pelts –
He did not leave the lace, his gift from the lady;   2030
Gawain did not forget that for his own good.
Then he belted his blade about his bold haunches,†
And he dressed doubly round him that lady's token.
Neatly that knight swept it sweet round his waist,
So that girdle of green silk was all gaily displayed   2035
In splendour most rich on that royal red cloth.
But this girdle was not worn this way just for show,
Nor for pride in its pendants, though polished they were,
And even though glittering gold gleamed at its edges,
But to save himself when he might suffer death,   2040
And bare to bide danger with no blade or knife to
    fight with.
  With that bold man bound,
  He ventures out forthwith,
  And all those people of renown   2045
  He thanks often like his kith.

Then Gringolet was brought, who was great and huge,
And had been safe stabled in such a good way,
So to be prick for point, as was that proud horse.†
The warrior walks to him and looks him all over,   2050
And so gracious and soberly swears to himself:
'Here is a great household that thinks only of honour –
And the man who maintains them, he must have joy;
And that dear lady, through life, let love long betide her!
So when they out of charity cherish a guest,   2055
And hand out hospitality, may He reward them
That holds up high heaven, and also you all!
And if I might live upon earth for any long while,
I shall if I can freely work to reward you.'
Then he steps up in the stirrup and strides aloft;   2060
He takes his shield from his servant and lays it on his shoulder,
And thus he goads Gringolet with his gilt heels.
And he starts on those flagstones, standing no longer
    to prance;
  With his guide mounted then,   2065
  Who bore his spear and lance.
  'May this castle Christ commend,'
  He said and, blessing all, advanced.

The drawbridge was brought down and the broad gates
Were unbarred and both their leaves then borne open.   2070
The noble blessed himself, fast crossing the boards.
He praises the porter – who knelt before that prince
Commending good God to bless that day and Gawain –
And he went on his way with only his guide,
Who would teach him the turns to that terrible place   2075
Where he should receive that most pitiless slice.
They bear by woodland where boughs are bare,
They climb by cliffs where the cold clings.
Beneath all high heaven it was ugly thereunder:
Mist mizzled on the moor, melted on the mountains;   2080
Each hill had a hat, like huge hackles of mist.
Brooks boiled and broke on the hills all about,
Shattering white on the shores where those riders pushed down.
Well winding was that way they went through the woods,
Till the time comes that season for the bright sun to rise and   2085
     not hide.
  They were on a hill most high,
  The white snow lay beside;
  The guide who rode close by
  Bade his master to abide.   2090

129

'Dear one, I have brought you thus far at this time,
And now you are not far from that noted place
That you have so specially sought and spurred after.
But I shall say to you truly, since I know you well,
And as you are a lord that I love with my life: 2095
If you would do as I ask it would serve you better.
The place that you press to is held to be perilous;
In that wasteland is one who is worst upon earth,
For he is stiff and is strong and he loves to strike many,
And more mighty than any man on Middle Earth,   2100
And his body is bigger than the best four knights
That are in Arthur's house, in Hector's or others.
He chooses by chance such that at the Green Chapel,
None passes by that place so proud in his arms
Who he does not deal death by sheer dint of his hand;   2105
For he is a mirthless man who shows no mercy,
Be it churl or chaplain who rides by that chapel,
Be it hermit, or monk, or any man else,
He thinks it quaint just to quell them as be quick himself.†
So I say to you surely as you sit in your saddle,   2110
Come you there, be you killed, as that knight does rule,
Trust me on this truly, even though you had twenty lives
          to spend;
     He has dwelled here long of yore,
     Bent on battle, friend;   2115
     Against his blows full sore
     You may not so well defend.

'So, good Sir Gawain, let the giant alone,
And get you gone some other way, by God's will!
Take yourself to other lands, let Christ care for you, 2120
And myself I shall head home again, and here vouch
That I shall swear by God and by all His good saints,
So help me God, on holy relics and by all other oaths,
That I shall always leave your secret loyally untold
And none shall ever find you fled from any fellow I know.' 2125
'Great thanks,' said Gawain, but grudging he said:
'Indeed you are worthy who would do me such good
As loyally let this lie, I know that you would.
But no matter how well held, if I did pass here,
Found afraid and did flee in the form that you say, 2130
Then I be a knight coward never to be excused.
So I will to that chapel, whatever chance may befall,
And talk with that terror any tale of my choosing,
Whether well be our words or woe, as fate shall
     behave; 2135
  Though he be a stern man
  That stands with club or stave,
  I know our Lord God can
  His loyal servants save.'†

'Well,' said that other man, 'now you cast your own spell,　　　2140
Such that brings your own end nigh unto yourself,
But if you like your life little, I shall not keep you longer.
Here, put your helm on your head, take your spear in your hand
And ride down this road here by yonder rock side,
Till you're brought to the bottom of this blighted valley.　　　2145
Then look a little on the land, on your left-hand side,
And you shall see in that swale that self-same chapel,
And that burly noble whose glebe it keeps.
Now goodbye in God's name, Gawain the noble!
For all the gold in this kingdom, I will not go with you,　　　2150
Nor be your fellow in these wastes one foot further.'
With this, that guide in those woods he wends his bridle,
Hit his horse with his heels as hard as he might,
Gallops over the land and leaves the knight there all
　　　　alone.　　　2155
　　'By God Himself,' said Sir Gawain,
　　'I will not gripe nor groan;
　　To God's will I true remain,
　　And to Him I give my own.'

Then he goads Gringolet and gathers the road,   2160
Shoves on by a scarp with scrub at his side,
Rides by that rugged bank, right to the dale.
Then he looked round about, he thought it most wild,
And sees no sign of residence nowhere beside,
But high banks all bleak upon both sides,   2165
And rough-knuckled knolls of rocks and stone;
Those scouts scratched the sky, it seemed to him.
So with that he hove to and withheld his horse,
And kept changing where he looked to chance on that chapel.
He sees nonesuch in no side, which he thought so strange,   2170
Seeing little on that land save a knoll as it were,
A bald bump by a bank, beside the brim river,
Which flushed about there by the force of its flow;
That bourn blubbered such there that is seemed to boil.
The knight spurs his charger and comes to that knoll,   2175
Gracefully alights and to a lime tree attaches[†]
The reins which he ties round a rough branch.
Then he bears to that barrow and he walks about it,
Debating with himself what it might be.
It had a hole at one end and on either side,   2180
And overgrown with grass that grew everywhere,
And was all hollow within, naught but an old cave,
Or a crevice of an old crag, he could not find the words
      to tell.
   'Oh, Lord,' said the gentle knight,   2185
   'Have I found the Green Chapel?
   Might I around midnight
   Hear the Matins of the Devil?'

'Now in truth,' said Gawain, 'it is windswept here;
This oratory is odious, overgrown with herbage;   2190
As well beseems the one wrapped in green
To deal here his devotion in the ways of the Devil.
Now I feel it is the Fiend, in my five wits,
That has dealt me this destiny to destroy me here.
This is a chapel of mischief – let doom chance befall it! 2195
It is the worst-cursed church that ever I came in.'
With his helm on his head, his lance in his hand,
He roams up to the roof of that rough home.
Then he heard from that hillock, in a hard rock
Beyond the brook, in the boulders, a wondrous bad noise. 2200
What! It clattered in the cliff as if it should cleave it,
As one upon a grindstone was grinding a scythe.
What! It whirred and did whet as water at a mill;
What! It rushed and it rang, horrible to hear!
Then, 'By God,' said Gawain, 'that growling I trust,   2205
Is arrayed so to reverence me and my rank, as befitting,[†]
   by plot;
  Let God do His work, I know
  Regret is futile in this spot.
  Though my life I might forgo,   2210
  These noises I fear not.'

Then the knight called, crying full loud:
'Who is master of this homestead that would tryst with me?
For now is good Gawain got here as arranged.
If anyone will, come here at once,   2215
Either now or never, to be done of your business.'
'Abide,' came the words from the bank above his head,
'And you shall have hastily what I promised you.'
And, still rolling, he rapidly razored the while,
Whetting and whirling before he would come down.   2220
Then he clambers by a crag and crops up from a hole,†
Whirling out of some dark way with a foul weapon,
A Danish axe, and new-edged, to yield duly that blow,†
With a burnished blade bent right down to the shaft,
Filed on a file-stone, four foot large –   2225
Made no less by that lace that gleamed full bright.†
And that guardian in green was geared as first seen,
Both the look and the legs, the locks and the beard,
Save he now fared on foot, and strides firm on the earth,
Setting steel to the stone as he stalked beside it.   2230
When he wound to the water, and not wishing to wade,
He hopped over on his axe and boldly strides,
Loud bellowing on a big field that was broad all about laid
    with snow.
  Sir Gawain that knight he greets,   2235
  But would not bow too low;†
  That other said, 'Now, sir, sweet
  To our tryst you have been true.'

'Gawain,' said that green man, 'God looks on you!
I wish you warm welcome, sir, to my place,   2240
And you have timed your travels as a true man should,
And you know well the covenant kept between us:
At this time twelve months gone, you took as were told,
So I should at this New Year repay as so held.
And we are in this valley, truly alone,   2245
There are no peers to part us, we can press as we like!†
Have your helm off your head and have here your payment;
Brook no more debate than when I bowed for you
When you whipped off my head with just one whack.'
'No, by God,' said Gawain, 'that grants me life,   2250
I begrudge you not one grain for the grimness that falls,
But strike with just one stroke and I shall stand still;
I will not refuse you, so work as you would like
        to fare.'
    He leaned his neck and bowed,   2255
    And showed those shoulders bare,
    And let as if not cowed;
    Tremble? He would not dare!

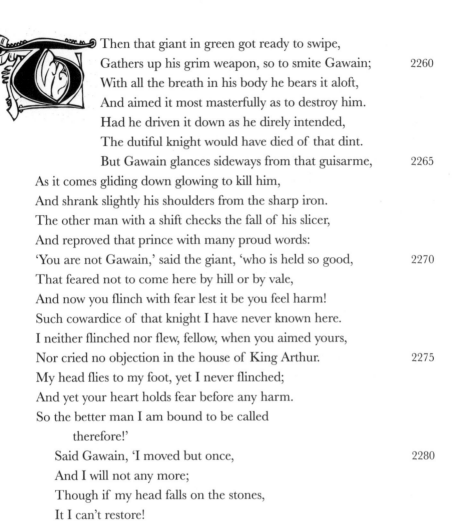

Then that giant in green got ready to swipe,
Gathers up his grim weapon, so to smite Gawain;   2260
With all the breath in his body he bears it aloft,
And aimed it most masterfully as to destroy him.
Had he driven it down as he direly intended,
The dutiful knight would have died of that dint.
But Gawain glances sideways from that guisarme,   2265
As it comes gliding down glowing to kill him,
And shrank slightly his shoulders from the sharp iron.
The other man with a shift checks the fall of his slicer,
And reproved that prince with many proud words:
'You are not Gawain,' said the giant, 'who is held so good,   2270
That feared not to come here by hill or by vale,
And now you flinch with fear lest it be you feel harm!
Such cowardice of that knight I have never known here.
I neither flinched nor flew, fellow, when you aimed yours,
Nor cried no objection in the house of King Arthur.   2275
My head flies to my foot, yet I never flinched;
And yet your heart holds fear before any harm.
So the better man I am bound to be called
        therefore!'
    Said Gawain, 'I moved but once,   2280
    And I will not any more;
    Though if my head falls on the stones,
    It I can't restore!

'But, man, be brisk, and bring me to the point;
Deal me my destiny and do it out of hand,   2285
For I shall stand that one stroke, and start no more
Till your axe has hit me; you have here my word.'
'Have at you then,' said that other, and heaves it aloft
And he waits in wrath as if he were wild;
He moves the axe masterfully, yet not touching that man,   2290
He checks his hand quickly lest any harm happens.
Gawain fittingly bides it and moved not one limb,
But stood still as a stone or more like a stump
That is anchored in rough ground with one hundred roots.
Then the man in the green said, mouthing his mischief: 2295
'So you have your heart back? I am ready to hew.
Now may all that high knighthood which Arthur placed on you
Keep your neck from this stroke, if it counts for aught!'
Gawain with grim fury and anger then said,
'Why thresh on, wrathful one, you threaten too long,   2300
I happen in your heart that you have not the guts!'
'Forfend,' said that fellow, 'so fiercely you speak!
I will no longer delay nor let light of your errand
      right now!'
    Gawain stands ready for that strike   2305
    And frowns in lip and brow;
    No wonder that he disliked
    That naught would stop that blow!

Gawain stands ready for that strike
And frowns in lip and brow;
No wonder that he disliked
That naught would stop that blow!

He lifts lightly his slicer and let it down fair
With the edge of its blade just by the bare neck.   2310
Though he hammered heartily, it did no more harm
Than skim him on that side, just piercing the skin.
It snipped the skin sharply where sits the white flesh,†
So that fresh blood shot to earth right over his shoulders.
And when that noble sees his blood bright on the snow   2315
He sprang forth spare-footed more than a spear's length,
Hoists his helmet with haste and casts it on his head,
Shot his shoulder suddenly beneath his fair shield,
Brings out a bright sword and boldly he speaks –
Not since being a boy, and born of his mother,   2320
Was he never in this world one half so happy –
'Be gone with your blows, big man, bait me no more!
I've had my stroke in this homestead without striking back,
And if you hit me more, I shall reply readily,
And give greedily again, that you may trust – and   2325
        more so.
    Just one stroke in this brawl –
    Our deal made you owe,
    Forged in Arthur's hall –
    So stop your hand now!'   2330

140

That stout man stood back and rested on his axe,
Set the shaft on the shingle and leaned on the sharp edge,
And looked at that lord who had come to his land,
How defiant and dauntless that doughty one stands
Armed full and fearless; in heart he likes him!　　　　　　2335
Then he mouths out merrily with much stance and statement,
And with a ringing delivery he said to the lord:
'Bold knight, be not angry on this our battleground.
No man here has misused you, nor been without manners,
Nor been unkind to that covenant shaped at your king's court.　　2340
I hit you with one stroke and so I hold you well paid;
I release you of all other rights which remain.†
If I had bashed you as bound, as perhaps was my duty,
Then I would have harmed you with more anger and wrath.
But first, with a minor blow, I mirthfully menaced you,　　　2345
I ripped you with no rend, as was right and proper
In honour of that faith we fixed on the first night,
When you truthfully by our terms did trustily give me
All your winnings and gains, given as good men should.
My other miss proffered was for the next morning,　　　　2350
When you kissed my wife comely, and her kisses you gave me.
For both those days I bid two blows and gave not my axe
　　　real use;
　A true man true repays,
　He need fear no dreadful muse.　　　　　　　　　　2355
　On the third day you betrayed
　So your neck I slight abused.

141

'For it is my weave that you wear, that woven girdle;
My own wife gave it to you as I would well know.
Now I know well your kisses and your conduct also,　　　　　2360
And of my wife and her wooing, I wrought that myself!
I sent her to assay you, and truly I think
You are the most faultless fellow that ever went forth.
As a pearl by a dried pea is surely more precious,
So Gawain, in good faith, seems by other good knights.　　　　2365
Yet you lacked a little and were wanting in loyalty;
Not because of no woven work, nor wooing neither,
But for the love of your life, so the less I blame you.'
That other stout man stood a great while in study,
So aggrieved with grim guilt that he gryed within;　　　　2370
All the blood of his breast blushed in his face,
That he all shrank for shame at the words that were shed.
The first words which our fellow formed from his mouth:
'A curse upon cowardice and coveting both!
You breed villainy and vice that destroys knightly virtue.'　　　2375
Then he caught of that knot and he loosens its coils,
Flings blushing that belt to that other noble:†
'Lo! There's a false thing, foul luck befall it!
For fear of your axe, it taught me much cowardice,
And denounced me as covetous to forsake my character,　　　2380
My largesse and loyalty, which belong to all knights.
I am now faulty and false, I who always was fearful
Of treachery and untruth – may both be blighted with sorrow
　　　and shame!
　　I confess, Green Knight, stood still,　　　　　2385
　　That I am sinful and defamed,
　　Let me understand your will,
　　So my future steers from stain.'

142

Then that other lord laughs and lovingly said,
'Any harm I had from you, I hold wholly atoned.   2390
You are confessed fully clean by knowing of your faults,
And taking open penance from the point of my edge,
I hold you polished of your plight, as purged and as clean
As if you had been sinless since you were first born.
And, sir, I give you this gold-hemmed girdle;   2395
Since it be green like my gown: Sir Gawain, you may
Think often how we threaped when you do throng forth
With your peerless princes, this being a pure token
Of the Challenge of the Green Chapel for all chivalrous knights!
And you shall in this New Year come again to my dwelling,   2400
And we shall revel in the remnants of that rich feast
    just been.'
  Then he beckoned fast, that lord
  And said, 'With my wife I deem,
  We shall now make true accord,   2405
  With she who was your sweet foe keen!'

'No, truly,' said the knight, and removing his helmet
He holds it with honour, and thanks the high man.
'I have stayed long enough, so good blessings befall you,
And may He well reward you who bestows all honour!   2410
And commend me to your courteous and comely wife,
Both herself and that other, my both-honoured ladies,
Whoso cleverly beguiled this knight with their craft.
But it is no fair wonder that a fool is made foolish
If through womanly wiles he is so won to sorrow,   2415
For so was Adam on earth with one so beguiled,
And Solomon with his women, and Samson often –
Delilah dealt his doom – and David thereafter
Was bewitched by Bathsheba and suffered bad fortune.
As women's wiles bewitched them, so I deem it be better   2420
To love them a lot and believe them but little, if man only could.†
For these men were the fairest that fortune did favour;
High above many others that under rich heaven
     have mused.
  And all these were bewiled   2425
  By women they amused.
  So if too I am beguiled
  I think I should be excused.

'For your girdle,' said Gawain, 'may God thank you!
I will wear that with goodwill, not for its gold worth,   2430
Nor its smoothness of silk, nor its swinging pendants,
Nor for worship of its wealth, nor its wondrous weaving,
But as a sign of my sinfulness I shall see it often,
And when I ride in renown, it shall speak my remorse
Of the frailty and fault of a flesh so corrupted,.   2435
How it be enticed by the pustules of sin;
And thus when pride shall prick me for my prowess at arms,
Just one look at this love-lace shall lessen my heart.
But one thing I would know, if it did not displease you;
Since you are the lord of this land that I've lived in,   2440
With your will and worship – may the Good Lord reward you
That upholds all heaven and sits up on high –
By what name are you known, I ask but no more?'
'I shall tell you that truly,' that other said then.
'Bertilak de Hautdesert, I am hailed in this land,†   2445
By might of Morgan le Fay, that dwells in my house,†
Who by cunning and practice and by crafts well-learned,
And the magic of Merlin, much of which she has knowledge –
Through some long time ago holding doting full dear†
That magical wizard as will know all your knights   2450
    the same;
  So Morgan the goddess
  Therefore is her name:
  There is none of great highness
  Who she cannot make tame –†   2455

'She worked me in this way to go to your hall
For to assay the surquedry, if it be so grand,†
That speaks of the great renown of the Round Table.
So she weaved this adventure to wrack all your wits,
And to grieve Guinevere and get her to die   2460
With gazing on that giant who spoke like a ghoul
With his head in his hand before the high table.
That is she, the old lady, that is at home;
She is even your aunt, Arthur's half-sister,
The duchess' daughter of Tintagel, that dear Uther later   2465
Had Arthur thereby, who is now your high king.
Therefore I urge you, lord, come to your aunt,
Make merry in my place, my household all loves you,
And I would as well, man, by my own faith,
As a good man below God, for your great virtue.'   2470
But he refused and said no, he would in no way.
So they encroach and kiss, and commend each other
To the Prince of Paradise and part right there in
        the cold;
    Gawain on his horse clean   2475
    To Camelot he bustles bold,
    And the knight entirely green
    Wanders off somewhere untold.†

They wakened well in that dwelling when the great were aware
Good Gawain was come back; they thought it glorious.
The king kisses the knight, and the queen also,
And then many other sure knights sought to hail him.

Wild ways in the world Gawain now rides
On Gringolet, free that grace had granted him life.   2480
He harboured often in homesteads and also in the fields,
With many ventures in the vales and victories as well,
Which I do not intend to recount at this time.
The wound was now healed that he wore on his neck,
And he bore that belt blinking all thereabouts,   2485
Arrayed as a baldric bound by his side,
That lace tied below his left arm with a knot,
As a sign he was tried and taught of his fault.
And thus that knight, he comes to court all safe and sound.
They wakened well in that dwelling when the great were aware   2490
Good Gawain was come back; they thought it glorious.
The king kisses the knight, and the queen also,
And then many other sure knights sought to hail him,
And asked freely of his faring and he tells them fairly,
And recounts all the costs to his care he had borne: 2495
The challenge of the chapel, the cheer of the knight,
The love of the lady and lastly that lace.
He showed them the naked nick in the neck,
He had claimed for disloyalty at the hands of that lord in
      his game;   2500
    He was tormented so to tell,
    He groaned with grief and blame;
    The blood in his face did well,
    In showing of his shame.

'See! Lord,' said the knight, as he handled the lace, 2505
'This is the band of blame I bear on my neck,
This is the blazon of loss I have claimed
For the coveting and cowardice that I did catch there.[†]
It is a token of untruth showing I am detected,
And I must always wear it while long may I last; 2510
For man may hide his sin but unhappen it he can't,
For once it is attached, it will never untwine.'
The king comforts the knight, and all the court also,
Laughing loud at it lovingly, and so agreed
Those lords and ladies that belonged to the Table, 2515
That each member of the brotherhood a baldric should have,
A band of bright green crossed all about him,
So sweetly to wear for the sake of Gawain.
This was to declare the renown of the Round Table,
And all who wore it were honoured thereafter, 2520
As the best books of romance all do describe.[†]
Thus in the days of Arthur this adventure did betide,
As all the British books do bear witness to thereof.[†]
Since Brutus, that bold noble, first began here,
After the siege and the assault at Troy, in truth, 2525
    did cease,
  Many adventures here before
  Have unfolded such as this.
  And may He that bears the crown of thorns
  So bring us to His bliss! 2530
    Amen.

HONY SOYT QUI MAL PENCE.[†]

For man may hide his sin but unhappen it he can't,
For once it is attached, it will never untwine.

NOTES

For references, see 'Some Further Reading'.

1–14 *Troy* ... *treachery* ... *Aeneas* ... *Britain*. W. R. J. Barron, in his 1974 edition (revised 1988), says that these lines establish Britain's place within the story of Troy as described in Virgil's *Aeneid*, but also prepare the reader for potential deception. J. R. R. Tolkien, in his 1936 Middle English edition, has suggested that the Gawain-poet was drawing specifically from references to the trial of Aeneas as described in Guido della Colonna's *Historia destructionis Troiae*, where Aeneas aided Antenor in the betrayal of the city to the Greeks but sought, out of compassion, to protect princess Polyxena from being sacrificed on the tomb of Achilles. Antenor's subsequent betrayal of this plan, which resulted in the exile of Aeneas and his followers, is perhaps the treason referred to here in the opening lines, although it is not clear whether Aeneas himself is seen as the traitor.

The words 'tried for his treachery, the truest on earth' (line 4) might be seen as a legal trial (by which Aeneas is tried and then exiled for his truly treacherous deeds), or if we read as 'tried for his treachery, he was the finest of all men', then his exile is potentially unjust. Alternatively, since Aeneas isn't mentioned until line 5, the 'treachery' might actually be Antenor's, the result of which is Aeneas' exile. Barron says that the ambiguity of seeing Aeneas as a hero for his deception of the Greeks but as a traitor for his actions towards Troy may be reflected in the Gawain-poet's description of Britain as a land of both 'bliss and blunder' (line 18), a sort of damaged or cursed land. However, it seems that the Aeneids are able to found great cities elsewhere, implying they carried with them an honourable glory. Tolkien says that the use of the name Felix (fortunate, or happy) in line 13 to describe Brutus is unique to this poem and the reasons for it are obscure; it may lead to the concept that Britain was founded as a wondrous land in which great men later thrive, and if so, the role of Aeneas in trying to help Polyxena may also be reflected in the knightly value of honour towards women, as exemplified by the Round Table.

66–9 *reaching for presents … those that lost.* The Christmas game appears to involve the distribution of presents in which not everyone receives a winning prize, but there is joy irrespective of whether a person wins. This may be similar in concept to musical chairs. Barron suggests the game may be a derivative of the children's game of handy-dandy, also referred to in *Piers Plowman*. In the game, a child holds a gift hidden in a closed fist which he or she then moves between the other (empty) fist as a rhyme is chanted. Other players must choose which hand holds the item and, if correct, they keep what is revealed.

311 *surquedry.* See note to line 2457.

312 *Grendel-wind.* The manuscript has *grydellayk* or possibly *gryndellayk*, of Norse origins and implying fierceness. In *Beowulf*, we encounter Grendel, the ferocious demon of marsh and fen, and, in Old Norse, Grindil, the howling storm.

536 *All Hallows' Day.* 1 November, which only allows Gawain two months to travel to meet the Green Knight on New Year's Day. This, as shown by the references to North Wales, implies that the poet was well acquainted with the distances involved and was writing with known locations in mind. Tolkien tells us that Arthur regularly held court on this day so Gawain would have waited to leave until then. All Hallows' Day precedes All Souls' Day, when the Faithful Departed are celebrated and when Gawain himself departs on Arthur's behalf. The poet may have intended this to be a deliberate metaphor which his audience would have relished.

552 *the Duke of Clarence.* This title was held by Lionel of Antwerp, second son of Edward III, until his death in 1368, and when Lionel died without issue, it was awarded to Thomas of Lancaster, the second son of Henry IV, in 1412. Richard II, as second (legitimate) son of the Black Prince, might have become Duke of Clarence had not his elder brother, Edward, died in 1370.

601–2 *peytral … crupper.* If these are items of horse armour (see 'Glossary of Armour'), *paytttrure* and *cropore* in the manuscript, their inclusion implies a later style of armour than Gawain's (lines 569–89). A simpler explanation may be that both terms refer to the relevant harnessing of the front and back of the horse. This would explain the array of red nails as decoration and would be more logical and in keeping with the known fashions for war horses in England at this time.

606 *stapled … stuffed within*. Thick padding was stapled into the helmet itself for comfort and to cushion against the resonance of violent blows.

624 *pentangle … that noble prince* Gawain's emblem, the pentangle, is interpreted as a five-pointed star where, from any given point, two axes pass over and under the equivalent lines from other points of the star in what the poet calls an 'endless knot'. According to Andrew and Waldon, 'In the Middle Ages, the idea developed that Solomon's magic seal bore a six-pointed star made of two interlaced triangles; in the course of time, this became identified with the five-pointed star … which was used by Pythagoreans and other sects as a symbol of health and perfection.' The Gawain-poet has used the pentangle as emblematic of what he calls '*trawþe*', a term we might loosely understand as fundemental 'truth' or a state of godly perfection, integrity and honour. When he speaks of this truth 'by title that it has' he means 'by its intrinsic nature': *trawþe* is the definition given for fully balanced human perfection. In a contemporary reading, this state of perfection would serve as a foil to the eventual partial fall of Gawain in Fitt 4, even though we know from Fitt 1 that Gawain, impetuous and indeed brutal, is strangely at odds with the almost angelic truth of the pentangle. In such a light, we might even see the star as indicative of the conflict between religious zeal and human frailty – a key theme of the poem.

629–30 *English … Endless Knot*. The poet appears to be addressing an audience that speaks another language (probably French), although the poem has already been written in English. This may be a conceit adopted to add a perceived authority, as if the tale is told from an older original; perhaps the poet means to say 'in

Old English', referring to a local dialect or a linguistic strand now lost. Israel Gollancz, in his 1940 Middle English edition of the poem, also says there is no other reference on record to the phrase 'Endless Knot'; again the poet may, in referring to Celtic designs, be attempting to create an illusion of the story originating from a much older source.

637 *shield and coat.* Gawain's pentangle features on both his shield and jupon. Michael Strickland, in Anne Curry and Malcolm Mercer's *The Battle of Agincourt,* says that 'the wearing of such coat armour was a jealously guarded privilege', either acquired by ancestral right or as a privilege only granted by the king or a high lord. He also states that the public bearing of arms in this fashion was a statement of valour and that being seen to retreat on a mission while wearing such clothing was deemed unchivalric and shameful. Hence, Gawain's decision openly to display his arms on his journey revealed to his audience that retreat from his quest would not be acceptable (as they would have well understood).

661 *tracing my fingers.* The poet asserts that no chink in Gawain's five virtues could be found and that they are all interwoven with each other, impossible to separate. In the manuscript, he refers to a 'game' (*gomen*), whereby he cannot see at any stage where the star ends, which has been interpreted as trying to follow the line of the star with his fingers, and failing to find a break in all the links.

681 *dubbed ... pride.* The manuscript is difficult to interpret, yet the poet's use of a dubbing (or appointing) metaphor shows his genius, contrasting noble dubbing by sword with beheading by ghoulish axe.

690 *the book does say*. A popular conceit of mediaeval romance is that the writer asserts a source for the story, enhancing credibility (see note to lines 629–30). With the creation of the *Domesday Book* (1086) in particular, written evidence replaced oral history as a statement of verifiable truth. For further reading on the growth of the power and influence of writing, see M. T. Clanchy's, *From Memory to Written Record*.

701 *wilderness of Wirral*. This section is the only one to describe known geographical locations in North Wales. It is thought that the Holy Head refers to the holy well (the wellhead) of St Winefride at Holywell (rather than Holyhead on Anglesey). The site was a well-known pilgrimage destination with a story that tangentially reflects Gawain's fate. St Winefride was beheaded by a Welsh prince, Caradoc, when she refused his advances. The holy well sprang up where her head fell and she was later miraculously restored to life by her maternal uncle, Saint Beuno. The Wirral was deforested by decree in 1376; it is clear that the poet knew of it by name, area and content; some have argued that this dates the poem to before that document.

770 *tied in many trees*. Some translators have seen this as a description of a large timber palisade in the manner of an early Norman wooden castle. However, the distance involved ('more than two miles') and the later description of a castle built in the latest style, suggest that the palisade is more like a thorny hedge around a park. Imparkment was a recognised symbol of status and power. Typically, mediaeval deer parks were contained within a shallow earthen bank topped by thick hedges. The reference to 'pinned full thick' (*'pyned ful þik'*) in line 769 can thus be interpreted as

hedge-laying in the traditional manner, where young trees are cut with billhooks, bent over and pinned to the hedge bank with wooden stakes. For a detailed discussion, see *The Medieval Deer Parks of Hertfordshire* by A. Rowe.

786 *deep double ditch that defended that place*. The description of the castle – a palace or 'place' – that follows is convincing: see the appendix 'In Search of Hautdesert'.

789 *corbels*. The original manuscript refers to *table* ʒ, which may mean cornices, corbels, string-work or machicolations.

792 *arrow loops that locked full clean*. Possibly wooden shutters designed to protect archers shooting from the embrasures (gaps) between the merlons ('teeth') of the crenellations on the wall walk.

802 *pared out of paper*. Barron cites Chaucer's description in *The Canterbury Tales* of '*bake-metes and dissh-metes ... peynted and castelled with papir*'. It would seem that the tables of feasts in wealthier households were often decked with paper castles and other decorations. The poet's knowledge of this hints that he may well have operated at the highest levels of society.

820 *the broad gate*. Typically large gates had within them a wicket gate, a smaller door in one of the leaves for regular foot passage. The gate 'gaping' suggests the opening of the gates in their entirety to allow the free passage of horses and indicating warm, and honourable, welcome. There is a well-preserved wicket gate within a larger wooden gate at Chepstow Castle, Monmouthshire.

881 *ermine*. The manuscript reads '*Alle of ermyn in erde, his hode of þe same*', which might translate as referring to ermine (the pelt of a weasel), acting as an earth or background for the bright colours of the rest of Gawain's clothing. Gollancz (1940) suggests this may be a scribal error and the word intended was *enurnde*, or adorned, rather than *erde*, or earth. See *blauner* in the 'Glossary of General Terms'.

897 *penitential fare*. The household has offered Gawain a meal comprising mainly of fish, reflecting that Gawain is on his own penitential journey, in places fasting en route (line 694), to atone for his rashness in taking the challenge at Camelot. We might also view his quest as honouring a pact with the Devil (in the form of the Green Knight); his journey is a penance for this act.

927 *love-talking*. Sir Gawain is able to craft his language for enjoyment rather than seduction. The constant references to Mary and his belief in the beauty of Guinevere above others suggests that he is intended to be pure (although, as we learn, vulnerable to 'womanly wiles', line 2415), and possibly celibate.

934 *comely closet*. Probably the lord's pew, reserved for him and his wife. Often in mediaeval churches such pews were mounted above the main chapel on a raised balcony.

943–5 *fairest in face … more bewitching*. The description of the lady as more attractive than Guinevere imbues her with great power, unsettling the reader by suggesting temptation in a place (the chapel) which should be spiritual and pure. There is no direct reference to Guinevere's infidelity in the poem although in the original '*and wener þen Wenore'* ('more beautiful than Guinevere') may be an obscure reference or pun.

964 *model matriarch.* This description of the older of the two women is strange, considering that she is later revealed to be Morgan le Fay; perhaps it is meant to be ironic. If she is Arthur's half-sister, she is shown as somewhat older than him.

972 *bowing full low.* The matriarch, for reasons which become apparent later, is held in great esteem. The poet is preparing us for the way the story develops.

975 *claim his acquaintance.* Sir Gawain is asking the two women to get to know him more.

979 *spiced cakes.* The word in the text is *spyceʒ*, which may be translated as 'spices'. Barron uses 'sweetmeats'. A further possibility may be some kind of scented incense brought to the room to burn in the fireplace or chimney (line 978).

985 *mirth be made at that Christmas time.* A parallel for the games and adventures in Camelot a year earlier. The game invites the winner to gain the honour of wearing the lord's hood (line 983) as a reward for creating the most laughter. This may reflect mediaeval carnivals, when servants become lords and the lords their servants.

1006 *served graciously as by their degree.* This passage reflects social protocol, with different levels of society being served according to rank.

1022 *St John's Day*. The feast of John the Evangelist on 27 December, or the third day of Christmas. It is notable that events occur in threes regularly throughout the poem (the hunting scenes, the temptations of Gawain and the three axe blows at the end). The poet may simply have included this reference to build suspense as we draw nearer to Gawain's meeting at the Green Chapel on New Year's Day. However, St John's depiction in Western art is often one of androgyny with an appeal to women; this has particular relevance on line 1788 (see 'Arthurian Characters and Saints').

1026 *carolling*. Here festive dancing rather than the singing of carols. The guests clearly wanted to make as much of the holiday as they could, enjoying every last minute in celebration of Christmas.

1028 *did not dwell there*. This line reflects the close-knit community of landed knights and squires who most likely were the guests. At a time of increasing urbanisation in mediaeval society, holding such events may be seen as maintaining the 'old order' of things. M. J. Bennett (*Community, Class and Careerism*) has shown that landed families across Cheshire and Lancashire enjoyed intimate relationships with knights travelling to meet with each other not just socially but also to decide upon legal and administrative matters.

1030 *chimney*. The Middle English word *chymné* refers to an intimate fireplace within a chamber where private matters may be discussed, a useful literary device. A typical mediaeval chamber fireplace was inefficient and comprised merely a decorative opening behind which was a wide chimney leading straight to the sky (unlike a modern fireplace, which has a built-in smoke shelf before the open smoke chamber). To gain any warmth, people would have needed to sit right next to the fire itself; the poet's use of the fireplace device throughout the poem may reflect this behaviour.

1033 *that highest tide*. Christmas time.

1038 *may the High King yield you more*. May God grant you wealth and happiness.

1040–1 *high and low by right*. The chivalric code compels Gawain to honour his host, the lord of the castle, in recognition of his generosity.

1108 *sweet swap*. The agreement states that this swap shall be undertaken with honour and without prejudice: if one man's prize is better, there shall be no adjustment.

1116 *French refinement*. Although the use of English was common in courtly circles by the time of Gawain, this reference suggests that French influence in terms of courtly behaviour and fashion was still seen as aspirational or conventional.

1127 *Guests wishing to go*. Guests so inclined gather together early to go hunting with the lord; others make their way home as they wish.

1153 *Restrained by … beaters*. To constrain the hunt, men were stationed around the hunt field to drive the deer back towards the hunting pack by shouting at them.

1157 *the male deer*. To preserve the numbers of the herd, the lord has ordered that stags and bucks should be let through the blockades; hunting will focus on the hinds, female deer of three years or more.

1158 *'Hay!'* … *'War!'*. Shouts and exclamations made whilst hunting. 'Hay' may be a derivation of the French *haye*, or hedge; 'War' perhaps a shortening of wattles (see notes to lines 1168 and 1708).

1160–1 *arrows … whistled*. The word used by the poet for 'whistled' is *wapped*. Archers will be familiar with the sound made by arrows in flight, and in particular when they hit their target, and this word may well be onomatopoeic.

1162 *broad heads*. Hunting arrows, unlike the bodkin used in warfare, used broad heads and were designed to cause maximum damage and slow the animals quickly, not unlike a harpoon for whaling.

1168 *received*. The poet uses *resayt*, which is interpreted as a receiving station, presumably on the boundaries of the hunting area. The next line has *wattreȝ*, which we can interpret as the deer being driven down to the river to finish them off ('teased'). Such a scene is shown for boar hunting in the *Livre de Chasse de Gaston Fébus*, an illustrated contemporary hunting manual. The manual does not show deer themselves being driven to the water. It is tempting to see *wattreȝ* as 'wattles', a common technique whereby animals are driven towards ever-narrowing funnels, but the Gawain manuscript is unambiguous.

1195 *lurked*. The poet has *lurked*, which is correctly translated as 'concealed', so we could have the line: 'The lord lay concealed a full long while'. However, in line 1180 Gawain lurks in bed while the daylight shines on the wall, which does not suggest concealment, so *lurked* might simply imply lingering.

1199 *espy with my speech.* The manuscript reads: '*to aspye wyth my spelle in space quat ho wolde*'. *Aspye* is more realistically, if more clumsily, translated as 'to discover'.

1202 *signed himself with the cross.* Gawain makes the sign of the cross in the hope that this will deliver him safety and protect his virtue from the mysterious advances of the lady.

1219 *unpress your prisoner.* The lady is sitting on the bed so that Sir Gawain is trapped below the blankets and unable to move about. For a knight so renowned for his own prowess with women, he is powerless to act against the lady of the castle, which adds greatly to the eroticism of this scene.

1224 *hasp … your other half.* This might have two meanings: either the lady is sitting on the bed with an arm each side of him to trap him in the blankets, or she is saying she shall take both halves of Sir Gawain: the top which is visible and the bottom below the sheets. The contemporary audience would have huge enjoyment at Gawain's predicament.

1276 *you have chosen one better.* Sir Gawain tells the lady that she has chosen for herself a better man – her husband – but he is prepared to be her servant. The poet appears to be telling his audience that this is the best way to avoid temptation, no matter how great.

1307 *commend each other to Christ.* This line has a powerful sense of sin, perfectly balanced against what appears on the surface to be playful behaviour. In Gawain's case, he has a religious duty to avoid adulterous behaviour as well as a chivalric duty to honour his host, Lord Bertilak. In the lady's case, she appears to be challenging Christ himself. The change of tense after the kiss adds greatly to the sense of shame, as if Gawain is overcome with guilt and now seeks distraction.

1326 *the greatest in fat*. The fattest of the deer are sought by those of highest rank in the hunting pack.

1338 *through a little hole*. This exquisite detail is also captured in one of the scenes from the *Livre de Chasse de Gaston Fébus*.

1340 *gullet*. The throat; the manuscript reads '*and eft at þe gargulun bigyneȝ on þenne*'.

1347–8 *know it to be true by kind*. This description of butchering a deer may show that the poet had knowledge of other works, such as the source works for the (much later) *Book of St Albans* and *The Parliament of the Three Ages*. Whether he referred to them or wrote from his own observations, the writer clearly knew how to deliver expert description to his audience and enhance his credibility.

1352 *chined*. The manuscript reads *Bi þe bakbon to unbynde*. In modern butchery, chining is the process whereby meat is cut along the backbone of an animal.

1355 *the fee for the raven*. Gollancz (1940) alerts us to a quote from Turbeville: '*there is a little gristle which is upon the spoone of the brysket (i.e. at the end of the breast bone) which we cal the Ravens bone, bycause it is cast up to the Crowes and Ravens whiche attende hunters'*. It would appear to be a hunting superstition aimed at rewarding the carrion birds to bring future good luck. In modern Siberia, hunters listen for the sound of crows in the forest to help in locating prey; the 'fee' in this light may be seen as a reward for the crows' help.

1356 *either thick side*. The word in the manuscript is *ayper*, which might also be translated as 'both'.

1358 *fellow*. The huntsman are paid with portions of the kill, according to their rank and contribution.

1359 *hide of that fine beast*. Although the manuscript refers to a beast in singular, there would have been sufficient pelts laid out to service all the hounds.

1360 *leather of their paunches*. The stomach linings or tripe.

1395 *not in our foreword*. Gawain tells the lord that it is not part of their agreement to reveal where each other found their gifts (although it is notable that the lord apparently tells Gawain the whole story of the deer hunt). Again this points to the impression of sin and deception in Gawain's behaviour.

1403 *men by the wall*. Gawain and the lord have retired to a private chamber with its own fireplace. In such a setting, servants would have been on hand discreetly at a distance; much in the manner of servants at a modern state function.

1428 *heartening them*. The hunters chivvy the hounds with horn-blowing and loud shouting.

1440 *Long since from the sounder*. This boar appears to be grown old and ousted from the herd (the sounder); a loner, he is angry and still powerful notwithstanding.

1459 *heads hopped off*. The hide of the boar is so thick that arrows either prick lightly the outer flesh or simply bounce off it, enraging the beast yet further.

1509 *wrathful*. The Lady hopes Gawain will not be angry with her as she delicately tries to unlace his chivalric stance.

1513 *letters of arms*. The doctrine or practice of chivalry, a legal reference perhaps? (See next note.)

1515 *title and token and text of it works*. A titled token might be an illuminated letter at the head of a manuscript, suggesting the poet might have had a legal or administrative background.

1519 *bowers of their ladies*. The *boure* could refer to a private chamber or even the lady's bedroom. The lady appears to be suggesting an erotic outcome: she wants more from Gawain.

1584 *bright blade*. Boar swords, like boar spears, were items of significant size and weight, often with disproportionately large blades so to finish such a fierce animal swiftly and with maximum force.

1640 *one more he served there*. Gawain gives the lord the two kisses granted him by the lady.

1658 *sweetness*. The word is *semblaunt*, the making of expressions to the knight, encouraging him to respond to the lady.

1697 *Hunters unharnessed*. The hunters release the hounds from their harnesses.

1708 *hedges*. The hedges are most likely hurdles, situated to compel the fox to turn back towards the hunters, examples of which are shown in the *Livre de Chasse de Gaston Fébus*. This could then explain the 'hurdle' (*spenne*) in the following line. An alternative is that the hunting ground takes the form of a deer park, bound in by well-maintained wood-banks topped by thick hedges.

1739 *tresses*. The poet has *tressour* or hairnet. In the manuscript, one illustration shows the lady wearing a type of hairnet. Though the rest of her outfit is minimal she still wears jewellery, which is clearly linked to the process of seduction.

1741 *breast bare before and also behind*. The lady appears to be in a nightdress, with the addition of soft pelts adding to the erotic sense. There is also an element of passion creeping through; she could not – or did not want to – find time to dress.

1743 *Waves up a window*. The description of opening the window in the manuscript – *Wayveʒ* (throws) up – is confusing. The lady may be opening the window to give a metaphorical coolness to the heated seduction or is drawing up a wooden board or shutter, perhaps to close the view from any prying eye.

1769 *not her knight so mind*. The lady now is at her greatest power, and Gawain must now rely on Mother Mary to hold fast on his behalf.

1795 *mourn in this realm*. The lady is distressed that Gawain has no other lover yet still rejects her advances. She is also trying now to make Gawain feel guilty; she asserts that he is condemning her to a wilderness of lost love. It is as if this last kiss is the taste by which she shall remember him, unkissed by him for evermore. The mediaeval 'Reply of Friar Daw Topias to Jack Upland' merges Cupid and Robin Hood (Dobson & Taylor):

> *On old Englis it is said*
> *Unkissid is unknowun;*
> *And many men speken of Robyn Hood*
> *And shotte nevere in his bowe …*

The kiss has a profound power and is the ultimate measure, just below a sexual relationship, of delicate intimacy.

1809 *hampers*. The word is *maleȝ* (baggage). The line reflects how noblemen would have travelled, well supplied with servants and materials. Gawain's journey to his audience would have seemed both dangerous and lonely. The convention of travelling alone with little baggage is not unusual in mediaeval literature, for example in Chrétien de Troyes's *Perceval*.

1856 *jewel*. This reference is similar to the bejewelled circlet about the knight's helmet; jewels offer a protection against danger.

1884 *Doomsday*. The day of judgement. There is a stark contrast between the solemnity of the lord's chapel and the previous seduction scene. We are not told whether Gawain confesses his deceit with the girdle. If he is bound to the lady, he must deny God. If he confesses to the priest, he has denied the lady. Gawain's 'merriness' (line 1885) – the happiest he has been since he arrived (lines 1890–92) – appears to argue that he has confessed to the priest. This would also help absolve him of sin in the minds of his audience and also explains Bertilak's forgiveness later. Francis Ingledew writes in his 2006 book on Sir Gawain that an audience would also have understood the connection between Doomsday and New Year's Day (when Gawain must face his own judgement by the Green Knight). New Year's Day is also the Feast of Circumcision in which, he says, Gawain 'experiences a figurative circumcision with its significations, which include the new life effected by baptism'.

1937 *sufficient and sweetly as he should be able*. At first glance, '*as saverly and sadly as he hem sette coupe*' implies a good-natured embrace, but a deeper reading suggests a certain hesitation, reflecting Gawain's inner knowledge that he hasn't handed over all of the gifts he received.

1941 *openly paid*. Here, for the first time, Gawain lies to the lord; a critical moment.

1944 *foul fox fur*. The fur is a token of recognition of the equally tainted gift that Gawain offers: three kisses bespoiled by the deception of the girdle.

1944 *the Fiend take these goods*. The pelt is only fit for the Devil because of the deception, perhaps?

2018 *rattled of their rust*. This description of cleaning armour is literal and metaphorical. Gawain's armour has been significantly exposed to damp and needs to be shaken in sand and cleaned of small rust blemishes. It is also a shaking loose of Gawain's accreted past as now he cleanses himself and his soul for the task ahead.

2023 *finest man from here to Greece*. The most handsome knight in the world. The manuscript reads: '*þe gayest in-to Grece; þe burne bede bryng his blonk*'. Greek culture and philosophy had undergone a renaissance in the early to high Middle Ages, and the poet views Gawain as the perfect knight, refined, pure and elegant; the apogee of chivalry.

2032 *bold haunches*. The poet uses *balȝe* to describe Gawain's upper legs. The meaning is uncertain but is usually translated as 'smooth'. Contemporary funerary monuments show knights with smooth upper legs, between the base of the surcoat and the top of the poleyn. The poet may allude to the upper legs as unarmoured by plate and therefore smooth or bare of armour. The word is used again (a *balȝ berȝ*, a bald bump, line 2172) to describe the surface of the Green Chapel, although there it is closer to its original derivation, the Norse word *bali*, or smooth bank, a grassy strand by a riverside (Gollancz, 1940).

2049 *prick for point*. Responsive to spurs and ready for action.

2109 *be quick himself.* 'Quick' meaning 'to be alive'; in context, the Green Knight enjoys killing as much as he enjoys living.

2139 *His loyal servants save.* Here deceit speaks loudly. Gawain trusts in God to save him at his hour of need. The guide, perhaps again part of a design to test Gawain's virtue, seeks to tempt him to flee. Gawain's response, delivered *gruchyng* (grudging, line 2126), is honourable, but he also knows that he will be assisted by false means. Gawain asserts that God will save all his loyal servants but the audience is aware that he is entering this battle with a darker force to protect him, the green girdle.

2176 *lime tree.* In *Silva* Archie Miles says that in German folklore, justice was carried out under a lime tree and that Hildegard of Bingen used the lime tree to ward off the plague. Did the poet deliberately choose the *linden* for symbolic reasons or use it simply as a generic word for a tree?

2206 *arrayed so to reverence me.* Beheading was the execution of choice for nobility; Gawain implies he is to be executed according to his rank in society.

2221 *crops up from a hole.* The Green Knight emerges suddenly from the landscape; indeed, he has yet to cross the river to the chapel. See the appendix 'In Search of the Green Chapel' on features of a karst landscape.

2223 *Danish axe.* The manuscript refers to a Dane's axe. Although this might imply a large double-handed axe of the type used in earlier centuries, the description is similar to the guisarme that the Green Knight uses in Fitt 1 (lines 208–20) new-edged. The manuscript has *dyȝt*, meaning 'prepared'. The blade was ground for added sharpness on the grinding wheel to deliver its blow with greater ease.

2226 *lace that gleamed full bright.* The manuscript is unclear: '*Hit waȝt no lasse, bi þat lace þat lemed ful bryȝt*'. It might be descriptive of the axe being next to a lace or girdle; a comparative way of judging the length of the blade against a known object (the girdle); a reference to the green girdle and thereby an invocation or calling to the girdle to help Gawain; or an attachment to the axe in much the same way as the lace attached to the axe described in lines 217–20. My wording implies that the axe was so fierce that its own huge power could not be diminished by that of the lace.

2236 *would not bow too low.* A joke: Gawain is wary of bowing lest he be summarily executed.

2246 *press as we like.* The poet appears to be referring to a set of rules whereby two combatants can be parted. This may relate also to 'battle bare' (see 'Glossary of General Terms').

2313 *white flesh.* The manuscript has *schyre grece*, shining or white fat. We encounter a similar description during the beheading of the Green Knight (line 425), although his flesh is green. If, as Ingledew suggests (see note to line 1884), Gawain's encounter is connected to the Feast of Circumcision, the delicate nature of the wound and the blood dropping from it onto the pure snow carries a strong religious connotation and one of rebirth from sin.

2342 *all other rights*. Although 'rights' can be rules, the legal language infers knowledge of these terms: the Green Knight is offering full and final settlement.

2377 *blushing*. The manuscript has *bropely*, angrily; the alliteration reflects both his anger and his shame.

2421 *if man only could*. Gawain consoles himself by saying he is not alone in being brought down by the charms of women. This stanza is at odds with the rest of the poem. Other works from the period include diatribes against women, but to have such an outburst here for the sake of literary convention seems extreme. Given contemporary events, and the possible role of the Gawain-poet as a poet–mentor to royal princes, it may reflect the decline of Edward III under the influence of Alice Perrers. Ingledew, in placing the poem earlier in the fourteenth century, suggests the outburst may also allude to the purported rape of the Duchess of Salisbury by Edward III as described by the chronicler (and propagandist), Jean le Bel.

2445 *Bertilak de Hautdesert*. Gollancz (1940) cites Hulbert's article ('The Name of the Green Knight: Bercelak or Bertilak', from *The Manly Anniversary Studies in Language and Literature*, Chicago, 1923) that Bertilak is an English translation of the French Bertolais: 'Hulbert suggests that the name is taken from Bertolais of the Vulgate Merlin (the Estoire de Merlin written in the thirteenth century), who becomes Bertelak in the English translation. Bertilak was the abettor of the "false Guinevere" in her second attempt to take the queen's place.' It is possible that a mediaeval audience, well versed in the Arthurian legends, would have been quick to understand the unveiling and relevance of Bertilak to this story.

The name Hautdesert, like that of Bertilak, only appears once in the poem. From the French, high empty place or wilderness, it evokes an isolated castle far from civilisation. As well as placing the castle in a magical land, its name also implies that it would be very difficult to find, further adding to its mystique.

2446 *Morgan le Fay.* The Green Knight suggests that he (as Bertilak) dwells at Hautdesert by the will of Morgan. It may be the case – as implied in lines 2454–5 – that the magical powers of Morgan le Fay could be those of a servant of the Devil and consequently, Bertilak's role in the poem is such that we might actually pity him. The word 'fay', Old French *fae* or faerie, may have a similar etymological origin to the Middle English word *fade* (line 149): '*He fered as freke were fade*' (translated here as 'He was a man like faerie clad').

2449 *doting full dear.* Another reference to men's weaknesses; in this case Merlin himself being brought low by the wiles of Morgan.

2455 *Who she cannot make tame.* Bertilak has already asserted that he holds his power through Morgan and his curious transmutation from human lord to Green Knight is almost – but not quite – out of his control. Seen in this light, we might consider the Green Knight's merciful treatment of Gawain at the end to be the soul of Bertilak himself fighting the evil by which he is entrapped.

2457 *surquedry.* An overweening pride or arrogance. In the manuscript it is spelled *surquidré*, which is similar in form to the Old French *surcuiderie* (Gollancz, 1940). While we might view it as part of Morgan's contempt for Camelot, the poet's audience might have seen it as reflection on the decline of Edward III's prowess or as broader criticism of the failing and arrogant court of Richard II. The contempt Morgan has for Guinevere may be a critique of the pure love Richard had for his wife, Anne of Bohemia.

2478 *Wanders off somewhere untold.* As at the beginning of the poem, the departure of the Green Knight is as mysterious as it is curiously melancholic. He doesn't return to Hautdesert but leaves almost as a lost soul wending his way in a hinterland between life and death – Middle Earth. He is a vehicle for exposing failure and folly; his personality and imbued characteristics compel us to reflect upon what he represents. His curious offer to take Gawain back to Hautdesert to meet his aunt is rightly refused, as for one last time the poet says that corruption and weakness must always be resisted and can appear at most unexpected moments.

2508 *coveting and cowardice.* Gawain handles the lace and could appear to be describing it as the band which he wears as a badge of shame. The poet masterfully also ties in the lace with the healed wound on Gawain's neck, implying the scar is a permanent reminder. Such wounds were well known in the Middle Ages, for example, the disfiguring facial wound suffered by Henry V at the battle of Shrewsbury in 1403. The poet's '*þis is þe laþe and þe losse þat I laȝt have*' (line 2507) is apposite, for the curved slit in Gawain's neck could well have resembled a laughing scar, permanently humiliating him and reminding him of the folly of his ways. The reference 'that I did catch there', could mean receiving the wound at the Green Chapel but, in this context, now makes more sense as the wound caught there, i.e. visible on his neck. The wound also acts as a gruesome rejoinder to the finessed five points of chivalric virtue on Gawain's shield, as proudly described in Fitt 1 (lines 619–65).

2513–21 *The king ... all describe*. It is curious that the Round Table adopts the green sash in celebration of Gawain's adventure. Read at face value, Arthur acts as a joyous king welcoming his knight errant back to the fold of Camelot and perhaps also seeking forgiveness for his own role in allowing Gawain to undertake the challenge. However, if the poem is read as an allegory of contemporary events in England, is the Gawain-poet making a deeper statement? Does the wearing of the sash mean we accept the monarchy come what may (the sash establishes legitimacy for the king and his court irrespective of sexual morality, usurpation or arrogance)? Or does it mean that we view the royal court with shame (the sash is a badge of pride and arrogance or a token of betrayal)? Either way, the sash can only be seen – as Gawain himself suggests when describing his scar – as a 'band of blame' (line 2506).

2523 *British books*. The chronicles of Britain, often called the Brut. The poet here draws us back to the authoritative matter on which he has built.

2531 *HONY SOYT QUI MAL PENCE*. The motto of the Order of the Garter of Edward III appears to have been added later and by a different hand. (It should read 'MAL Y PENCE' or, as rendered today, '*honi soit qui mal y pense*'.) It may have been added so that readers would reflect upon the Order of the Garter and the responsibilities of the king, whether Edward III, Richard II or Henry IV. It means 'shame be to him who thinks evil of it' – or, as is stated in the alliterative *Wynnere and Wastoure* in the only written example of the phrase in Middle English: '*hethyng have the hathell þat any harme thynkes*'.

GLOSSARY OF GENERAL TERMS

See 'Glossary of Armour' for military terms.

Assay A test of the deer; in line 1328 the deer are assessed for their quality, as being either fat or lean.

Baldric An ornamental belt; in line 621 used to hang the shield around Gawain's neck and shoulder.

Battle bare Either fighting in single combat or possibly a match without weapons, such as bare wrestling, as seen on the corbel frieze at Kilpeck church, Hereford and on the Bayeux Tapestry.

Blauner Ermine, made from the white winter fur of the stoat, with its distinctive black tip of the tail. Believed to be a corruption of French *blanc et noir*; the heraldic symbol for ermine is a white field with black flecks.

Bonchief Happiness, the opposite of mischief.

Bourn A stream, often in limestone country such as the Peaks, which is dry in summer but floods in the wintertime.

Branch The point where the windpipe splits to the lungs.

Doser or Dorser An ornamental hanging behind a throne or royal dais.

Ell-rod A physical measure of one ell. The English ell equated to a length of twenty nails. A nail, at 2¼ inches, was ¹/₁₆th of an English yard making an ell ⁵/₄ of a yard or 45 inches. The ell was a measurement of certain types of cloth imported from the low countries and ceased to be an English measurement in 1824. The reference to the ell-rod as a measuring stick may suggest the poet had knowledge of its use in the cloth trade.

Erber The first stomach of the deer.

Filidore A type of fine gold thread woven in luxurious cloth.

Foreword A treaty or agreement made in advance of deeds to come.

Groin In the manuscript, the word is *grayn*, meaning 'fork'. This may be where the blade meets the shaft of the axe, akin to a groin in a vaulted ceiling where two halves join together.

Gryed Gry is an old Lancashire dialect word for an inner ailment or fever. A tamer alliterative translation might be that 'he grieved within' although this would repeat 'aggrieved' (line 2370).

Guisarme A poleaxe with a large blade. The word is used several times, although the description is closer to a weapon known as a bardische. The illuminations to the original manuscript show a large-bladed poleaxe being wielded by Gawain. The blade is broad, similar to an executioner's axe; the choice of weapon may have been used by the poet to evoke the sense of horror.

Gules The heraldic term for red. The poet is familiar with heraldic terminology although he chooses to use the word 'gold' rather than 'or', its heraldic equivalent, in the next line (620).

Linden The linden or lime tree; the poet probably chooses the tree for alliterative reasons and is referring to trees in general shedding leaves in autumn. See note to line 2176.

Logres In modern Welsh, *Lloegr* is translated as England (or, in the past, England south of the Wash/Bristol Channel, although in Arthurian romance it may refer to Britain as a whole).

Middle Earth *Myddelerde* in the manuscript is seen as being between heaven and hell. The term originates from the German *middangeard*, or middle yard (or ground). The poet chose not to use *erde* (earth/ground, as he did in line 2098) and instead creates a supernatural sense to the existence of the Green Knight, rooting him firmly in the spiritual landscape of its intended audience.

Moot The word in the manuscript is *mere*, an appointed place. 'Moot' retains alliterative flow, and reflects ancient Saxon 'moots', where meetings were held to decide on key issues.

Nakers A type of mediaeval kettle drum.

Numbles The entrails or offal of a deer.

Prime One of the liturgical hours and a fixed time for prayer in the morning, around 7 a.m. To reach the Green Chapel at first light, Gawain wakes very early indeed, as he has to dress and travel the few miles to his tryst.

Rood The cross (line 1949); an interesting contrast to the Fiend mentioned by the lord (line 1944). This exchange would have had great significance to contemporary audiences, when religious themes and references had great power.

Threaps/Threap Lancashire dialect, meaning to argue. The word in the manuscript is *þrepe*, which is hauntingly similar and means the same.

Toulouse and Tharsian Rich silks from both places. They denote wealth and, in the case of Gawain's chamber (line 858), are a symbol of great hospitality: Gawain had been offered a room where no expense was spared.

Tryst A pre-defined hunting station in the forest. *Tryster* in the manuscript is a derivation of the Old French *tristre*.

Welkin The sky or the heavens. Its use here shows again the Gawain-poet's mastery in describing the landscape and the seasons.

Wodwose, wodwo or woodwose The wild men of the forest, frequently described in mediaeval literature. There is an interesting wild man at the feet of Sir Robert Whittingham (d. 1471) on his tomb at Aldbury in Hertfordshire.

Womb The abdomen, just above the waist of the Green Knight. He is clearly in good physical shape.

Worms A worm is a common term for a dragon. In North Wales, the name of the headland Great Orme (worm) reflects its position at the head of the winding river Conwy. There is also the Lambton Worm, a dragon that casts a curse over generations of the Lambton family, in folklore from north-east England; and Piers Shonks, the Hertfordshire dragon slayer, is described as having fought with a worm of the Devil in the lonely fields around the Pelhams.

GLOSSARY OF ARMOUR

The description of the knight's armour and horse (lines 573–618) is one of the key sections that help to assign an approximate date to the poem. The combination of plate, mail and padding strongly indicates the practice of the later fourteenth century (as indeed do the somewhat primitive illustrations in the Cotton Nero A.x manuscript). Contemporary funeral brasses with armour are also instructive for dating within a period of approximately sixty years. These include those for Sir John de la Pole at Chrishall in Essex (*c.* 1370), Sir John d'Argentine at Horseheath in Cambridgeshire (*c.* 1382) and Sir Thomas de Audley at Audley in Staffordshire (*c.* 1385). By the early fifteenth century, the style is still visible in such monuments as those to Sir Reginald de Cobham at Lingfield in Surrey (*c.* 1403) and Sir William de Burgate at Burgate in Suffolk (*c.* 1409), although by the 1420s, fuller armour has become the norm. Of particular interest is the magnificent tomb of Hugh de Calveley in Bunbury, Cheshire (*c.* 1394), which even includes a circlet, in the manner of Sir Gawain himself. It is interesting to note that the tomb of Sir Hugh was commissioned by Sir Robert

Knollys, who had significant connections with the Duchy of Lancaster; both may have been known to the Gawain-poet (see 'In Search of Hautdesert').

Aventail The mail skirt stapled to an open-faced helmet or bascinet (the type of helmet most likely to have been worn by Gawain). It extended completely from the area just below the ears, all around the neck and over the shoulders.

Braces Or more commonly vambraces; plate armour of the forearm.

Byrnie A mail shirt worn beneath an outer layer. Large mail coats (also called hauberks) were obsolescent by approximately 1410.

Caparison Typically a large cloth or blanket covering the horse at the front and rear, and usually bearing the heraldic device of the knight. In the poem it may refer to a decorative harness, embossed with golden nails (lines 602–3).

Circlet A decorative ring of cloth, usually padded and apparently bejewelled, around the top of a bascinet. It may have had an heraldic purpose to help distinguish knights in close combat or a supernatural relevance, designed to protect the wearer from danger or evil deeds. A similar description to lines 615–18 is given in the *Alliterative Morte Arthure*, which was written later than *Sir Gawain* in *c.*1400. In that poem, as King Arthur dresses to fight a mighty giant (lines 908–9), he puts on a circlet which is also decorated with jewels. The later tombs of Sir Hugh Calveley (see introductory note above) and Lord Bardolph (d. 1441) at Dennington, Suffolk, both feature circlets (but are not shown on the brasses mentioned above). It is thought that jewels were also believed to protect the wearer against poison (although it is curious that Lady Bertilak wears a jewelled headdress when she attempts her final seduction of Gawain, line 1738).

Couter A plate section protecting the elbows and allowing flexible movement.

Crupper Armour (or padding) to protect the rear of a horse (see note to lines 601–2). More simply it could refer to harnessing of the rear of the horse.

Cuisses Plate armour to protect the upper legs.

Greaves Plate armour to protect the lower legs.

Hauberk An armoured coat of chain mail. Gawain's would have been much smaller than earlier coats of *c*. 1100

Jupon A tight-fitting, often padded, sleeveless tunic covering the chest and hips. It often carried the heraldic arms of wealthier knights.

Mullets Small star-shaped decorations, derived from the heraldic term for the star, mentioned in relation to horses (line 169).

Paunce Armour for the lower body or paunch.

Peytral Armour (or padding) to protect the chest of a horse. More simply it could refer to harnessing of the front of the horse (see note to lines 601–2).

Poleyn Similar to the couter but designed to protect the knees.

Pysan A part of a suit of plate armour believed to be the gorget, protecting the throat; from the old French *pizanne* or *pisinne*. Its inclusion may push the date of the poem into the early 1400s.

Sabatons Articulated metal shoes to protect the feet.

Vrysoun In the manuscript, this word appears to refer to a cloth covering for the aventail. It is unclear why it would be *above* the aventail unless it formed part of a decorative cover. Usually such coverings, known as *lambrequins* or mantlings, flowed from the back of jousting helms (such helmets being significantly larger than a simple bascinet with aventail). The description of the rich embroidery suggests the item was for show, and it might be a kind of diminutive cloak, perhaps attached to the circlet. This appears to be suggested in the closure of the stanza (lines 615–18), when it implies it is attached round the crown with a circlet encrusted with gleaming diamonds.

ARTHURIAN CHARACTERS AND SAINTS

Sir Gawain and the Green Knight refers to characters in the Arthurian canon although, with the exception of Arthur, Gawain and Guinevere, most are mentioned briefly (such as Lancelot or Hector) or in a contextualised setting where the reader is expected to understand the power of the characters (Morgan le Fay and Merlin). The poem is set in an idealised chivalric King Arthur's court when the characters are 'in their first prime' (lines 54–5), and we are not told of the failings of Arthur or of Guinevere (though there may be veiled allusions). Instead we see the Round Table as the apogee of chivalry (albeit somewhat tainted by overweening pride), which may lead us to imagine that *Sir Gawain and the Green Knight* is an allegorical poem, created by a poet-mentor of great skill.

Major Characters

King Arthur Progeny of an illicit encounter between Uther Pendragon and Lady Igraine (wife of Gorlois, Duke of Cornwall); king and defender of a mythical Britain.

Bertilak de Hautdesert/Green Knight Bertilak lives at Hautdesert. There may be a veiled connection between him and Guinevere (see note to line 2445).

The lady Lord Bertilak's wife (or Lady Bertilak). Appears to be willing to follow Bertilak's orders in the seduction of Gawain. Her role is essential if it is seen as offering guidance to kings.

Sir Gawain Son of King Lot of Orkney and Lothian and of Arthur's sister, Morgause. Morgause is also sister to Morgan le Fay, so Gawain is a nephew of Arthur and Morgan.

Queen Guinevere Wife of King Arthur. In the poem she is shown as virtuous and noble and the epitome of womanhood, although she is hated by Morgan le Fay, as becomes clear at the end.

Morgan le Fay A fay, or faerie/sorceress; Arthur's half-sister and, as the daughter of Lady Igraine and Gorlois, duke of Cornwall, Gawain's aunt. Whereas Arthur is shown in his prime, Morgan appears to be aged.

Minor Characters

Agravain of the Hard Hand Gawain's brother; known as a fierce knight rather than a chivalric one.

Bishop Baldwin Baldwin (sometimes of Brittany) appears in a number of romances; including in the *Alliterative Morte Arthure* of *c.*1400.

Bedevere One of Arthur's finest knights; guardian of Excalibur in the *Alliterative Morte Arthure*.

Bors Son of King Bors of Gannes. Younger brother of Lionel, cousin of Lancelot; a leading figure in the romances.

Dodinal de Savage (of the wild) A lover of hunting; in some stories one of Arthur's best knights.

Eric (also known as Erec) a leading knight of the Round Table, given great repute by Chrétien de Troyes in *Erec and Enide*.

Hector Possibly a reference to Hector, son of Priam, in the stories of the Trojan Wars or, more likely, Sir Ector, adoptive father of King Arthur.

Lancelot After Arthur, the most famous character in the canon; there is no mention here of his adultery with Guinevere.

Lionel Elder brother of Bors, son of King Bors of Gannes.

Lucan the Good Lucan the butler; loyal to Arthur to the end.

Mador de la Port A minor knight; the 'doorkeeper'.

Merlin The wizard whose magic enabled Uther Pendragon to disguise himself as Duke Gorlois in order to sleep with Gorlois's wife, Igraine of Tintagel, to beget Arthur.

Yvain Son of Urien and Morgan le Fay, subject of Chrétien de Troyes's *Yvain, The Knight of the Lion*.

Saints

Saint Giles The patron saint of cripples; injured by a stray arrow intended for a hind in a hunt.

Saint John Saint John the Apostle. Barron says that by tradition he is dedicated to celibacy. Saint John is often shown in Western mediaeval art as androgynous, someone who could appeal both to men and women. Contemporary audiences may well have been amused by the reference to Saint John (line 1788) as Gawain finds himself in difficulty against Lady Bertilak while simultaneously being seen of knightly virtue by her husband.

Saint Julian This may refer to Julian of Antioch, who suffered numerous tortures; Julian of le Mans, who ended a drought by planting his staff in the ground, causing water to flow; or

Julian the Hospitaller, who was deceived into thinking his wife was adulterous.

Saint Peter The keeper of heaven's gate. As Gawain stands before Hautdesert after his perilous journey (line 813), the contemporary audiences may well have found the reference to Saint Peter amusing.

IN SEARCH OF HAUTDESERT

It is generally accepted that *Sir Gawain and the Green Knight* was written at the close of the fourteenth century. Indeed, its detailed description of the castle of Hautdesert – a palace or 'place' – is an accurate depiction of a new type of lordly homestead being built in England during this period. It is also, perhaps, a description of a 'perfect' rather than an actual castle, in the manner of the magical buildings often described in some works of the Arthurian canon. Yet it contains references which indicate that the Gawain-poet may well have conflated a range of actual buildings he had seen and that serve in some way to help define his travels in, and knowledge of, the British Isles, and these castles might also assist us in understanding who the poet was.

Certainly, his description of features, such as chimneys, conical roofs and the decorative corbelling/cornice work applied to the walls, are of a building of the later Middle Ages. We are not introduced to a keep or donjon but instead are presented with a hall, towers and chambers in perfect, balanced form. Bertilak does not live as a military lord but resides in a castle built as a grand home. Such decorative castles were prevalent in the later Middle Ages. Indeed, some commentators consider Hautdesert in the manner of the castles so wonderfully depicted in the *Très Riches Heures* of the Duc de Berry, for the castle as an aesthetic statement or even magical place in a rural landscape has increasingly gained acceptance. Some castles, such as Bodiam in Sussex, actually had a viewing platform from which visitors could marvel at the owner's magnificent creation. Bodiam also benefited from a contrived approach whereby visitors were compelled to appreciate the castle's magnificence by circumnavigating the building before entering it across a bridge which appeared to float upon the shallow waters.

In describing Hautdesert, the Gawain-poet may indeed have been thinking of Bodiam when he depicts the castle rising from the water and seeming to be 'pared out of paper', a common descriptive device. If we accept that the poem was written in the closing decade of the fourteenth century, of castles acquiring a licence to crenellate from the king in this period, only Bodiam, which was granted its licence in 1385, would seem to match the description. It is still seen today as the apogee of a mediaeval castle in England. Its builder Edward Dalyngrigge fought in France under Sir Robert Knollys, a Cheshire knight whose coat of arms commemorating their ties can still be seen at the castle. This establishes a fascinating possible connection with the north-west of England, the probable home of the Gawain-poet, although he introduces some other features which are not present in Sussex.

Hautdesert's double ditches limit us to only a few candidates in England, if prehistoric hill forts and Roman sites are excluded. Sheriff Hutton in Yorkshire features a partial double ditch (possibly in the form of a processional way) and was granted its licence to crenellate in 1382; it certainly stands out in the landscape, although it does not rise above the water as described by the Gawain-poet and was not remotely situated. More striking in terms of being in a high and remote place – as the name Hautdesert implies – is Helmsley, also in Yorkshire. Its location is conceivable as a distant castle in a wilderness, offering a warm reception to the traveller. However, its twin ditches are (and were) dry, unlike those described in the poem. While the barbican, another feature mentioned, is sizeable at Helmsley (unlike that at Bodiam), the use of the word in the poem (line 793) may be misleading. A barbican is a defensive outwork protecting a castle entrance, yet it is unclear whether the poet is referring to this or is using the term to describe the castle walls as a whole.

Finally, the description of finials (line 796) – *fylyoles* in the manuscript – reflects the design cues of a high Gothic palace or even a cathedral. Such details do appear on the crenellations of wealthier castles such as at Chepstow, but are also present on the remaining tower at Doddington in Cheshire, which is indeed finely decorated as described by the poet. However, little remains of that castle otherwise to suggest a link to Hautdesert. The subsequent description of these finials as having 'conical caps' (line 797) implies a second possibility: the towers carrying bartizans, or small watchtowers. Helmsley retains two bartizans on its keep, although they are square. Helmsley's belong to an earlier age, and the impression given in the poem is of a castle very much in the latest style.

What other candidates exist? If the poem is set in Cheshire then candidacy for Hautdesert as an *actual* place is not strong. The county has few castles of architectural significance; the one at Chester being too urban to be relevant. The royal stronghold at Beeston, perhaps the finest Cheshire castle, is on a plain which is visible for many miles and rises high above the landscape with views over to Wales, South Lancashire and the Peak District. Originally sited on an ancient hill fort as an assertion of status in the landscape rather than for defence, Beeston impresses even today, especially when viewed from the side below its towering great crag. Richard II is said to have visited the place, depositing much of his personal treasure there prior to travelling to Ireland in 1399. It does have two ditches, but that to the outer ward is indistinct, and neither it nor that to the inner ward encircle the castle (which is protected on two flanks by steep hillsides and cliffs) nor were these ditches ever full of water. Indeed, if the poet were describing Beeston, it is surprising that he makes no reference to its dramatic location, while Hautdesert emerges in a somewhat melancholy way from the woodland through which Gawain travels, much in the manner of that of the Fisher King in Chrétien de Troyes's *Perceval*.

Beeston may be relevant as a localised setting for King Arthur's castle, as a fictional Camelot in the mind of the audience. In line 59 Camelot is situated on a hill so the poet may have placed the entire story in a north-western administrative setting, much in the way that Edward III created his own Round Table at Windsor. Beeston's significant position in the Palatinate of Chester cannot be discounted, particularly if we consider the Gawain-poet, as poet–mentor, writing for significant national figures. The castle's visibility from the lofty heights of the Staffordshire Roaches – the land of Lord Bertilak – adds a magical frisson to the story; it is almost as if, out there in the wastes, Bertilak – like Satan – has been exiled from the great and the good.

What about castles in Staffordshire, Derbyshire and possibly Shropshire? There are few promising candidates. Beyond the county town of Stafford, Staffordshire boasts few larger castles;

Stafford itself is an earlier structure than that described by the poet and began life as a motte (mound) and bailey castle, albeit a significant one. Dudley is an urban castle with buildings of various dates. Tutbury has two outer baileys separated by a single ditch with two banks which appears to lead to the main castle, matching the poet's original description (line 786) of a *'depe double dich þat drof to þe place'*. However, modern interpretations suggest the poet's original words mean 'encircling and defending' rather than 'leading to' the castle. But neither Tutbury nor Dudley are contiguous new builds and neither is bound by water.

Derbyshire has fewer candidates still, for while the remote, hilly location of Peveril is appealing, its architecture is too primitive, and its main feature, a small keep, is far too unsophisticated to be granted any credibility. Whittington in Shropshire, once surrounded by lakes and water features, may have been familiar to the poet. although the architecture is from an earlier period as far as we can tell, and would not have been in the style he described. The castle, according to D. J. Cathcart-King, in *Castellarium Anglicanum*, was also 'in need of repair' by 1375 and so would be unlikely to have contained admirable contemporary features. Other large castles in the county (for example, Clun, Ludlow and Shrewsbury itself) do not match the refined homogenous construction described by the poet and are either too early in construction and layout or have distinctive features which are not described in the poem. None is possessed of a double ditch and all are in towns. The majority of the county's castles reflect its place as a marcher county bordering Wales; much of its castle stock has its origins in the Norman period.

Perhaps the only conclusion we can reach with any sense of certainty is that Hautdesert is based on several castles of significance and relevance to the poet rather than descriptive of any particular one. He has conflated them and employs his creation in the way that other poets have done in the Arthurian canon: a fantastic place, possibly an ideal castle, combining features the poet thought of as being indicative of a building of high status and nobility. It glows with magic, melancholy and menace in the manner of these tales, yet it speaks a silent language of its own to enable identification, for the significance of Hautdesert lies in the fact that some of its features may well have been drawn from castles of the poet's acquaintance and which therefore might provide some clues to his identity.

Edward Dalyngrigge, the builder of Bodiam in 1385, had significant disputes with the Duchy of Lancaster prior to a rapprochement. It could well be that our poet, in some form of administrative capacity, travelled frequently to assist in the management of this dispute. We might imagine him as working under John of Gaunt, protector of Richard II during his minority. Had the poet travelled more widely, he may have been familiar with the great watery lakes at Leeds Castle in Kent, which was also the place where Richard's future queen, Anne of Bohemia, stayed on her arrival in England. Castles in such grand settings would surely have impressed themselves on the poet's imagination.

Contrarily, the poet may also have had more direct connections with the Bolingbroke camp. When Bolingbroke returned from exile from abroad, he did so via North Yorkshire, travelling from Pickering westwards and no doubt passing via the high and remote country of Helmsley. Sheriff Hutton is also in this area and was owned by Ralph Neville, a convert to Bolingbroke's cause, and son-in-law, through his second marriage, to John of Gaunt. Is it possible therefore that the poet knew and travelled with both parties – king and Bolingbroke – and preserved his anonymity as author in order to hedge his bets? If the poet worked within the court of the Duchy of Lancaster, he could of course have stretched across two camps: an apparent supporter of the king but with loyalty to Gaunt's son, Henry Bolingbroke.

Much of this is speculation, but the poet's observations do appear to reflect an insight based on a visual – rather than written – experience of the architecture he describes. Any traveller on royal, princely or ducal duties would have seen many places, which could have served to embellish the description of Hautdesert. Certainly, the best castles – those designed to impress in the landscape – used water as a defining feature. As well as Leeds Castle, we might also consider Kenilworth in Warwickshire, Framlingham in Suffolk and Caerphilly in Wales, all of which would have appeared as magnificent emblems of local power. Yet these must be considered too large, too magnificent for Hautdesert. It is a homestead, set within a park, palisaded about and full of every comfort from conical roofs to chimneys and chambers. This is very much a castle as house at a time in the Middle Ages when money was being invested from people returning from war, aspiring to make a name for themselves and perhaps trying to recreate some of the wonderful castles they had seen abroad.

Bodiam is an aspirational place in this manner: it combines all the latest features of castle building but does so as a pastiche of great castles rather than as a military fortress. The same might be said of other castles built as homes during this period, such as Nunney in Somerset or the reconstruction works at Caerlaverock in Scotland. While Nunney might be discounted on account of its size, Caerlaverock must be considered because of its two moats. Its proximity to the coast appears to discount it as a model (no reference is made to the sea in the poem), but it is unlikely that any one would ever forget its distinctive defences, including its machicolations (which could be like the corbels/cornice work referred to as *tablez* in line 789). Yet the bulk of what we now see at Caerlaverock is most likely of a later date. B. H. St John O'Neill, in his guide to the castle, describes these works as dating from the fifteenth century. Equally, its highly distinctive design is also notable by its absence in the Gawain-poet's work. 'In shape it was a shield', says the *Siege of Caerlaverock*, a poem of *c*. 1300 written in French by an official within the English court.

In many ways, therefore, Bodiam emerges as the castle most likely to have inspired Hautdesert, to be the base on which it was built. Its moat is broad, it creates a magical impact enhanced even more by a processional entrance route. It was also a brand new building in the later Middle Ages, built to a fresh plan and designed for comfort and living; even its moat was shallow and has been proven in recent years to have had limited defensive capability. It too has machicolations on its towers. Yet it is the fact that the poet may have visited on business which is perhaps its most intriguing aspect. The Knollys connection at Bodiam and the disputes between Lancaster and Dalyngrigge provide a compelling reason to suggest that the castle was in the mind of the poet; perhaps embellished by a visit to Caerlaverock (or reading a copy of the famous French poem about the seige in some lordly library). Despite Bodiam's proximity to the south coast and the threat of French invasion, its military capacity is limited. Removing the 'deep double ditch' from the description, the way Bodiam sits within its landscape today evokes more than any other place perhaps the magic of Hautdesert, sitting soft in its plain for the enjoyment of hunting and other great pleasures. Add to it the defences at Caerlaverock and it is almost a perfect candidate. Yet there is one further surprise that Bodiam has in store for us. In his groundbreaking work, *Castles and Landscapes*, O. H. Creighton describes how the approach to Bodiam was not just via a circumnavigation of its moat but also by a processional route between a millpond and another water feature. If we take the Gawain-poet's description of the ditches at face value, might now indeed these two features be 'the deep double ditch that drove to that place' instead of defended it?

So it is that we may conclude that Hautdesert was a place which was *almost* real and, indeed, may have been nearly so. It wasn't incredible in the way of those castles of earlier romances; it didn't have any magical bridges built of swords or glass, or resonate with the cries of a thousand maidens. It was very much a castle which would ring true to a contemporary audience; every feature described by the poet existed in one form or another in castles being built right then at the end of the fourteenth century. Hautdesert may have its home in the Staffordshire Roaches, but its inspiration lies much further afield in the statement pieces of warriors returning from the Hundred Years' War. It floats on water, magically reflected, and glistens like a welcoming home with warm fires and good company within. Hautdesert may not actually be Bodiam, but Bodiam, and similar homesteads being built in late-fourteenth-century England, most likely inspired it.

IN SEARCH OF THE GREEN CHAPEL

When Gawain finally confronts his nemesis, he must do so at the Green Chapel, a site so feared that even Gawain's guide will not take him there. It is seen as a place of evil deeds – '*Com ʒe þere, ʒe be kylled, may þe knyʒt rede,*' says the guide (line 2111) – and certainly when Gawain arrives, he sees it as a 'chapel of mischief' (line 2195) – a chapel of doom. As the poet draws Gawain and his guide nearer, he builds the suspense first by describing the wickedness of its owner, then by making the guide try to dissuade Gawain from going and finally, by having the guide turn back out of fear. Gawain then descends into the valley and even now no building is seen, save a '*lawe*' or low – a barrow or smooth-sided knoll (line 2171). Finally, he arrives at the chapel to find it is 'naught but an old cave' (line 2182). This place has become not a religious building – a hermitage perhaps – but is instead a place which is overgrown with grass and appears to enter into the bowels of the earth: the home of the Devil. Did such a place really exist? Did the poet base his creation on somewhere known to him?

It is widely believed that the Green Chapel was known to the Gawain-poet, although opinions vary as to the inspiration. In all likelihood, it is a conflation of different places in the Staffordshire Roaches and southern Derbyshire Peaks, all of which combine to provide the perfect exterior, interior and ultimate location for this *'corsedest kyrk'* (in my text, 'worst-cursed church', line 2196). The most popular choice is the wonderful crevice in the cliff at Lud's Church at Gradbach, near the village of Flash in Staffordshire. Here the visitor will find, hidden among the trees on the valley side, a small stone bearing the name of the place and a narrow path that seems to lead into only a gap in the rocks. On entering, however, we are greeted by a steep descent into a narrow passageway through the rock face, which is – as the poem says – overgrown with herbage (line 2190); its sides are over thirty feet high; and it has a pervasive atmosphere of dread. Some indeed have claimed that it was here that Lollards gathered in the fourteenth century to practise their own anglicised form of religious service, far from the prying eyes of religious authority. But apart from the location and its putative associations, all similarity ends. Lud's Church has no roof; it is on the side of, rather than in, a valley; it is invisible from afar; nor does it stand beside by a boiling brook (line 2174), although there is a river a short distance away. While Lud's Church overwhelms in terms of the impression it makes, it does not stand out in the way the poet describes.

At Wetton Mill on the Manifold Valley, we find a much stronger candidate. Situated incongruously above a teashop beside the river, the cave shelter at Wetton Mill does indeed resemble the mound the Gawain-poet describes. It is visible from some distance away; it is not a cave within a cliff but a cave within a lump (possibly the remnants of a much greater cliff side); dating evidence found inside it apparently suggests that the cave was in use from the Palaeolithic through to the mediaeval period. Today part of the roof has collapsed and the entrances on either side – as described by the poet – are not evident; there is one main entrance and a much smaller one. It is possible that prior to the collapse there may have been other entrances; there is evidence of water flowing through the rocks at some distant period, a feature typical of the geology of karst landscapes. Since water has created passages within the rocks throughout this valley, the Green Knight could indeed emerge as if through a hole, as the poet relates (lines 2221–2). Certainly the landscape of Wetton Mill enables us to place the drama of the final scene at the Green Chapel within a plausible geographical context. The valley is intimate; it is possible for us to imagine here the Green Knight shouting from above to Gawain, as he stands on top of the roof of the chapel. We can see him crossing the river here and walking towards the cave. We might even imagine the Green Knight speaking from the gaping maw of Thor's Cave, further down the valley (not mentioned by the poet).

Yet we are compelled also to consider the way the Gawain-poet describes the chapel as a '*lawe*' or barrow, which suggests somewhere much simpler than the natural rocky mound at Wetton Mill. We do not have to travel far to find evidence of barrows that might have inspired him: at Arbor Low, the 'Stonehenge of the North' which sits on Middleton Moor just north of Ashbourne. While there is no cave, we do find, in nearby Gib's Hill, a barrow set within a plain – from here the visitor can see for miles in all directions. Arbor Low itself also offers elements of possibility; not least in its entrances on either side. Located near to a Roman road, the barrow and Arbor Low itself would have been both visible and well known to inhabitants of these uplands in the Middle Ages and being man-made would surely have inspired a fear of the unknown in the minds of contemporary folk. If there was any such lonely church where the Devil may worship, these two ancient features – little understood by scholars at the time – could well have inspired its creation.

So where was the Green Chapel? If the Gawain-poet knew this area well – which his intimate descriptions of the landscape appear to suggest – then it is possible he was inspired by visits to all three of these places: Lud's Church, the ancient caves of the Manifold Valley and Arbor Low. Yet to travel across the area would not have been a simple task in the Middle Ages; indeed, it is difficult even today to see all three places easily in a short space of time. So as it is likely that the Gawain-poet was a person of some standing who moved about with others, either on official business or in accompanying a rich lord on hunts in the wilderness, we can imagine that, just as the Gawain-poet created the magical castle of Hautdesert by conflating information gleaned from wide-ranging travel across the land, so too the Green Chapel is also a conflation of familiar places. Hence, today's traveller in search of the Green Chapel should plan a visit to the southern peaks and can in two days take in the sites of Lud's Church, Wetton Mill (and Thor's Cave) and the evocative Arbor Low. Only then can one truly say – as far as it is possible to know – that one has walked in the footsteps of Gawain-poet and seen for oneself where the Green Knight's mighty axe did rise and fall in its testing of Gawain.

SOME FURTHER READING

I have listed a range of titles which I have found to be useful in my own work on the poem and this list, though not comprehensive, will provide an excellent starting point for a reader new to the Gawain-poet. Some of the books are tangential, yet all are relevant to a contextual understanding of the poet, his work and the period in which he lived. Included are some of the more well-known student and scholarly works, many of which contain excellent bibliographies of their own.

Editions of the Poem

Andrew, M. & Waldron, R.: *The Poems of the Pearl Manuscript* (London, 1978)

Armitage, S.: *Sir Gawain and the Green Knight* (London, 2007)

Barron, W. R. J.: *Sir Gawain and the Green Knight*, revised edition (Manchester, 1998)

Gollancz, I.: *Sir Gawain and the Green Knight: Re-edited from MS Cotton Nero A.x in the British Museum*, Early English Text Society (Oxford, 1940)

Gollancz, I.: Introduction to *Pearl, Cleanness, Patience and Sir Gawain – Reproduced in Facsimile from the Unique MS Cotton Nero A.x in the British Museum*, Early English Text Society (London, 1923)

Tolkien, J. R. R. & Gordon, E. V.: *Sir Gawain and the Green Knight* (Oxford, 1936)

Related Studies

Bennett, M. J.: *Community, Class and Careerism – Cheshire and Lancashire Society in the Age of Sir Gawain and the Green Knight* (Cambridge, 1983)

Brewer, L. E.: *Sir Gawain and the Green Knight – Sources and Analogues* (Woodbridge, 1973)

Burrow, J. A.: *A Reading of Sir Gawain and the Green Knight* (London, 1965)

Horobin, S. & Smith, J.: *An Introduction to Middle English* (Edinburgh, 2002)

Ingledew, F.: *Sir Gawain and the Green Knight and the Order of the Garter* (Notre Dame, 2006)

Spearing, A. C.: *The Gawain Poet – A Critical Study* (Cambridge, 1970)

Turville-Petre, T: *The Alliterative Revival* (Cambridge, 1977)

Arthurian Romances and Mediaeval Poetry

Brock, E.: *Morte Arthure or The Death of Arthur*, Early English Text Society (Oxford, 1865)

Gardner, J.: *The Alliterative Morte Arthure, the Owl and the Nightingale and Five Other Middle English Poems* (Carbondale, Illinois, 1971)

Lacy, N. J. & Grimbert, J. T.: *A Companion to Chrétien de Troyes* (Cambridge, 2005)

Olschki, L.: *The Grail Castle and its Mysteries* (Manchester, 1966)

Raffel, B.: *Lancelot – The Knight of the Cart* (New Haven & London, 1997)

— *Perceval – The Story of the Grail* (New Haven & London, 1999)

Trigg, S.: *Wynnere and Wastoure*, Early English Text Society (Oxford, 1990)

General Reading

De Anthenaise, C.: *Le Livre de Chasse de Gaston Fébus* (Paris, 2002)

Armitage, E. S.: *The Early Norman Castles of the British Isles* (London, 1912)

Brown, R. A.: *Castles from the Air* (Cambridge, 1989)

— *English Castles*, third revised edition (London, 1976)

Cathcart-King, D. J.: *Castellarium Anglicanum, An Index and Bibliography of the Castles in England, Wales and the Islands* (Milwood, London & Nondeln, 1983)

Clanchy, M. T.: *From Memory to Written Record* (Oxford, 1993)

Creighton, O. H.: *Castles and Landscapes* (London, 2002)

Curry, A. & Mercer, M. (editors): *The Battle of Agincourt* (New Haven & London, 2015)

Davis, R. H. C.: *The Medieval Warhorse* (London, 1989)

Dobson, R. B. & Taylor, J.: *Rymes of Robyn Hood – An Introduction to the English Outlaw* (Stroud, 1989)

Duby, G.: *The Knight, the Lady and the Priest – The Making of Modern Marriage in Medieval France* (Paris, 1981)

Goodall, J.: *The English Castle* (New Haven & London, 2011)

Keen, M.: *Chivalry* (New Haven & London, 1984)

Macklin, H. W.: *Monumental Brasses* (London, 1913)

Miles, A.: *Silva, The Tree in Britain* (London, 1999)

O'Neill, B. H. St John: *Caerlaverock Castle* (Edinburgh, 1986)

Perroy, E.: *The Hundred Years War* (London, 1951)

Prestwich, M.: *Armies and Warfare in the Middle Ages – The English Experience* (New Haven & London, 1996)

Rowe, A.: *The Medieval Parks of Hertfordshire* (Hatfield, 2009)

Saul, N.: *Richard II* (New Haven & London, 1999)

Scott, M.: *Medieval Dress and Fashion* (London, 2007)

Thompson, M. W.: *The Decline of the Castle* (Cambridge, 1987)

— *The Rise of the Castle* (Cambridge, 1991)

ACKNOWLEDGEMENTS

I am indebted to my wife, Nicky Parker, who has tolerated my obsession with this poem for over five years during its translation. I must also in particular thank my wonderful old friend Nick Wray, who introduced me to the team at Unbound and has done so much to encourage the publication of this work. Nick has been a truly fantastic supporter, offering constant reassurance and enthusiasm even when it seemed the work could not progress; I simply cannot thank him enough for all that he has done. With this in mind, of course, I owe a huge debt of gratitude to Simon Spanton, Imogen Denny, Georgia Odd, Lindeth Vasey and the team at Unbound, who have worked diligently to bring this long project to fruition – not forgetting every single person who pledged financial support to enable this book to happen (and who are all named in the back of this book). I am also grateful to two of my oldest undergraduate friends from the University of York: Francis McCormack for his boundless knowledge of religious ritual and history; and Robert Jeffs who first alerted me to tense changes in the poem while reflecting on it over a beer beside the calm waters of Lake Coniston in 2013. I must also thank the Curwen Print Study Centre at Linton in the county of Cambridge who, with their fine tutors and superb equipment, made a printmaker out of me – and whose splendid Albion printing press gave birth to the images in this book. Mike Ashman, Dr Jon Banks, Suzy Richardson, Anne Sauntson and Jonathan Trower must also be mentioned as key drivers to get this translation over the line for a first successful reading at St James's Church, Stanstead Abbotts in Hertfordshire in 2016. Philip Kogan, with whom I worked at the publisher Kogan Page, is also due recognition – he always pushed me to take my work further and I hope this book is testament to his belief. Finally, it is an honour to name and thank my dear friends Nick and Julie Scarr, whose limitless enthusiasm for this project, including creating a wonderful environment for Christmas readings in their home, has done so much to shape and deliver its final outcome.

A NOTE ON THE AUTHOR

Michael Smith is from Cheshire. He studied history at the University of York, and printmaking at the Curwen Print Study Centre near Cambridge. This is his first book.

www.mythicalbritain.co.uk

SUPPORTERS

Unbound is a new kind of publishing house. Our books are funded directly by readers. This was a very popular idea during the late eighteenth and early nineteenth centuries. Now we have revived it for the internet age. It allows authors to write the books they really want to write and readers to support the books they would most like to see published.

The names listed below are of readers who have pledged their support and made this book happen. If you'd like to join them, visit www.unbound.com.

Drew Adams
Geoff Adams
David Adger
Ananda Allan
Lulu Allison
Will Anderson

Laurence Anholt
Sue Arthur
Tracey Ashman
Sarah Ashton
Gordon Askew
Tom Atkinson

James Aylett
Sonja Aylward
David Baillie
Simon Baines-Norton
Jon Banks
Andrew & Sarah Barnwell
Bob Beaupré
Samuel Becker
Armaiti Bedford
Emily and Elizabeth Bell
Terry Bergin
Karen Berrow
Adam Bertolett
Christian Bishop
Melanie Blacklock
Richard Blades
Graham Blenkin
Gretta Bloor
Jeannie Borsch
John Bothwell
Colin Bottle
Emily Boulter
Lesley Bourke
Alexander Bown
Lorna Bown
Mark Bowsher
Sophy Boyle
Nigel J Brewis
Marc Briand
Lindsey Brodie
Jack Brown
Margaret JC Brown
Steve Brown
Greg Bull

Steve Bulman
Matt Bunker
Rachel Burch
Joseph Burne
Geoff Burton
Aslan Byrne
Tom Callaghan
Debbie Cannon
Danese Carey
Anthony Carrick
George Carter
Martin Casimir
Sean Cerqua
Justin Cetinich
Rebecca Challis
Liz Chantler
John Luke Chapman
April Chase
Elizabeth Childs
Don Church
Juliet Clark
Iwan Clarke
Peter Clasby
Christopher Collingridge
Adrian Congdon
Charles Congdon
Will Conn
Andrew Connell
Julia Cook
Wendy Cook
David Cooke
Denise Cooper
Gaynor Cooper
Gina Cooper

Julie Cooper
Mark Cooper
Malcolm W. Corner
Jo Cosgriff
Tom Cox
Donna Cresswell
Steven George Critchley
Elizabeth Cross
John Crowther
Peter Cumiskey
Patricia Daloni
Dan Dalton
Catherine Daly
Nikoleta Damaskinou
Elizabeth Darracott
Jason Daub
Joe Davies
Andrew Davison
Steven Dawson
Deadmanjones
Jennifer Dellow
James Dempster
John Dexter
Kevin Donnellon
Stephen Dougherty
Bernadette Dunthorne
Paul Dunthorne
Frances Durkin
Suzanne Dwight
Graham and Chris Dyson
Christopher Easterbrook
Gareth Evans
Julie Evans
Michael Evans

Tom Evans
Doug and Jane Everard
Melanie Ewer
Diane Fairhall
Ida Falk
Alice Farrant
Virginia Fassnidge
Peter Faulkner
Charles Fernyhough
J Dudley Fishburn
Steve Fleming
Deborah Foster
Adam Fransella
Mark Gamble
Nicholas Garforth
Dan & Barbara Garner
Lynn Genevieve
David Gilbertson
Ben Glover
Dave Goddard
Maria Goldie
Giles Goodland
Marc Goodman
Stephen Grace
Eamonn Griffin
John Griffiths
Tim Griffiths
Peter Grundy
Michael Guilfoyle
Vincent Guiry
Daniel Hahn
Catherine Haig
Monica & William Haig
Stephen Hampshire

Vanessa Hamshere
Griselda Hamway
Jeanne E. Hand-Boniakowski
Kate A Hardy
David Harford
Cy Harkin
Tim Harper
Graham Harvey
James Harvey
Matthew Hay
Angus Head
Andrew Hearse
Emma Heasman-Hunt
Mark Heather
Margot Heesakker
Kate Heiss
Sam Hellmuth
Michael Heumann
Angela Hicks
Mary Hicks
Thomas Hillman
Tom Hirons
F & C Hobbin
Peter Hobbins
Joe Hoffman
Sebastian Horn
Mike Howarth
Alan Howe
Sara Howers
Karen Howlett
John Huddlestone
Matt Huggins
Bethan Hughes
Caroline Irwin

Paul Jabore
Daniel Jackson
Emma James
Mike James
Vic James
Aaron Janes
Helen Jarvis
Robert Jeffs
Lisa Jenkins
Rob Jenkins
David Jennings
Gregory Jennings
Simon Jerrome
Tristan John
Alex Johnson
Sarah Johnson
Duane Jones
Julie Jones
Michael Jones
Susan Jones
Paul Joyce
Abi & Anton Kadouchkine
Dave Keck
David Kellett
Aidan Kendrick
Lyn Kenny
Clive Kewell
Dan Kieran
Gregory Kindall
Jacqui King
Marc Kingston
Simon Kingston
Howard Kistler
Patricia Knott

Philip Kogan
Jacob Kvalvaag
Ketil Kvam
Mit Lahiri
Peter Lake
Taylor Lankford
Suzanne LaPrade
Alan Lee
Caroline Lee
Jenny Lemke
Rich Lennon
Alick Leslie
Carrie Lewis
Katie Lewis
Elizabeth Li
Laurie Liddington
Robert Liddington
Beverley Little
Gawain Little
Louisa Llewellyn
Kim Locke
Stephen Longworth
Isabell Lorenz
Nick Louras
Adam Lowe
Yvonne Luke
Joergen Lunde
Kara Maloney
Philippa Manasseh
Phil Manning
Keith Mantell
Juliet Marillier
Emma Marsden
Martine, Roos & Dees

Devon Martinez
John Massey
Niko Massouras-Townley
Brian Matthews
John Matthews
Marjorie Maws
Sasha Maximova
Janice McCaldon
Seth McDevitt
John A C McGowan
Thomasina McNaughton
Albertina McNeill
Stacy Merrick
Lucio Mesquita
Diana Metcalfe
William J. Meyer
Roger Miles
Liz Miranker
John Mitchinson
Edward Monk
Kirsty Morgan
Mark Morley
Daniel Morris
Jane Moseley
Bernard Moxham
Linda Muller
Doreen Munden
William Munn
Hugh N
Alix Nadelman
Debbie Nairn
Linda Nathan
Carlo Navato
Jeannette Ng

Kevin O'Connor
Ruth O'Leary
Karen O'Sullivan
Gregory Olver
Alan Outten
David Overend
Jussi Paasio
Scott Pack
Valentine Page
R D Palmer
Steph Parker
Phil Peacock
Lisa Pearce Collins
Phoebe Peberdy
Bianca Pellet
Clifford Penton
Penny Pepper
Hugo Perks
Jonathan Perks
Carolyn Perry
Neil Philip
Karon Phoenix-Hollis
Piggott's Daughter
Roger Pilgrim
Dr Andrew Plant
Hannah Platts
Stephen Pochin
Justin Pollard
Lin Pollock
Jennifer Porrett
Ian Preece
Jules Pretty
Malcolm Prue
Anna Pye

Ben Quant
Elizabeth L. Rambo
Susan Randall
Katherine Rasmussen
Sue Rattray
Samantha Rayner
Kerie Receveur
Simon Redman
Andy Reed
Katherine Reeve
Siân Renwick
Maggie Richardson
Suzy Richardson
Peter Rigby
Liam Riley
Adam Roberts
Mark Roberts
Simon Robertson
Mark Robinson
Kalina Rose
Adam Rosser
Elizabeth Rowlands
Irish Roz
Ian Rutherford
Lisa Ryan
Sioban Ryan-Togni
Emma Samuel
David Santiuste
John-Paul Sarni
Anne Sauntson
Julie Scarr
Nick Scarr
Seb Scarr
Arthur Schiller

Jenny Schwarz
Anne-Marie Scott
Rosemary Scott
Katharine Secretan
Matthew Sellen
Karen Selley
Margaret Sh
Eric Shaffstall
Tom Shakespeare
Faye Sharpe
Lloyd Shepherd
Kevin Shrapnell
David Shriver
Anthea Simmons
Peter Simpson
Alison Singhal
Sarah Singleton
Hazel Slavin
Barendina Smedley
Margaret Smith
Martin Smith
Nigel Smith
Peter, Hester & Kit Smith
Simon Smith
Stuart Smith
Colin Smythe
Jeremy Sowden
Pippa Sparks
Adam Sparrowhawk
Maureen Kincaid Speller
Linda Spence
Ann Speyer
Teresa Squires
Louise Sta Ana

Catherine Stals
Mary Steele
Nic Stevenson
Tena Stivicic
Andrew David Nigel Stocker
Toby Stone
Nina Stutler
Dan Sumption
Helen E Sunderland
Laurence Swan
Richard Swan
Adam Swann
Dave Swarbrook
Amelia Swift
Kirsty Syder
Catherine Syson
Georgette Taylor
Nicola Taylor
Paul Taylor
Stephen Teso
Gareth Thomas
Helen Thompson
Robert Thompson
Mat Tobin
Lindsay Trevarthen
Jonathan Trower
Mark Truesdale
David G Tubby
Lewis Tyrrell
Steve Uomini
David Valls-Russell
Michael Valls-Russell
Deborah Vaughan
Mark Vent

David Verey
Gary Vernon
Linda Verstraten &
  Pyter Wagenaar
Steve Wadsworth
Erica Wagner
Sally Wainman
Ben Walsh
Meredith Walsh
Ruth Waterton
Barbara Watkinson
Paul Watson
Dave Wealleans
Alexandra Welsby
Jane Wheeler
Janet Wheeler
Katy Whitaker
Russell Whitehead
Candy Whittome
Dean Wiegert
Thomas Wigley
Jim Wilkinson

Arnold Williams
Lisa-Jane Williams
Steve Williamson
Thom Willis
Frances Wilson
Juliet Wilson
Katherine Wilson
Leonard Wilson
Penny Raine Wilson
Peter Wilson
Catherine Winter
Howard Wix
James K Wood
Wendalynn Wordsmith
Nick 'Odour of Rice' Wray
Alex Wright
Rachel Wright
Peter Wylie
Rob Wyllie
Xelasoma
Meenu Yadav
Susan Zasikowski